NEW YORK REVIEW BOOKS
CLASSICS

TYRANT BANDERAS

RAMÓN DEL VALLE-INCLÁN (1866–1936) was born into an impoverished aristocratic family in a rural village in Galicia, Spain. Obedient to his father's wishes, he studied law in Compostela, but after his father's death in 1889 he moved to Madrid to work as a journalist and critic. In 1892 Valle-Inclán traveled to Mexico, where he remained for more than a year. His first book of stories came out in Spain in 1895. A well-known figure in the cafés of Madrid, famous for his spindly frame, cutting wit, long hair, longer beard, black cape, and single arm (the other having been lost after a fight with a critic), Valle-Inclán was celebrated as the author of *Sonatas: The Memoirs of the Marquis of Bradomín*, which was published in 1904 and is considered the finest novel of Spanish *modernismo*, as well as for his extensive and important career in the theater, not only as a major twentieth-century playwright but also as a director and actor. He reported from the western front during World War I, and after the war he developed an unsettling new style that he dubbed *esperpento* —a Spanish word that means both a grotesque, frightening person and a piece of nonsense—and described as a search for "the comic side of the tragedy of life." Partly inspired by his second visit to Mexico in 1920, when the country was in the throes of revolution, *Tyrant Banderas* is Valle-Inclán's greatest novel and the essence of *esperpento*.

PETER BUSH is an award-winning translator who lives in Barcelona. Among his recent translations are Juan Goytisolo's

Níjar Country and Teresa Solana's *A Shortcut to Paradise.* He is currently translating Quim Monzó's *A Thousand Morons* and Josep Pla's *The Gray Notebook* (forthcoming from NYRB Classics).

ALBERTO MANGUEL is an Argentinian-born Canadian essayist and novelist. He has written twenty works of criticism, including *The Dictionary of Imaginary Places* (with Gianni Guadalupi), *A History of Reading,* and *The Library at Night*; edited more than twenty literary anthologies; and is the author of five novels, including *News from a Foreign Country Came,* which won the McKitterick Prize in 1992. An Officier de l'Ordre des Arts et des Lettres (France), he has also been awarded a Guggenheim Fellowship.

TYRANT BANDERAS

RAMÓN DEL VALLE-INCLÁN

Translated from the Spanish by

PETER BUSH

Introduction by

ALBERTO MANGUEL

NEW YORK REVIEW BOOKS

New York

THIS IS A NEW YORK REVIEW BOOK
PUBLISHED BY THE NEW YORK REVIEW OF BOOKS
435 Hudson Street, New York, NY 10014
www.nyrb.com

Library of Congress Cataloging-in-Publication Data
Valle-Inclán, Ramón del, 1866–1936.
[Tirano Banderas. English]
Tyrant Banderas / by Ramón del Valle-Inclán ; introduction by Alberto Manguel ; translated by Peter Bush.
p. cm.
ISBN 978-1-59017-498-2 (alk. paper)
1. Dictators—Fiction. I. Manguel, Alberto. II. Bush, Peter R., 1946– III. Title.
PQ6641.A47T513 2012
863'.62—dc23
2012001138

ISBN 978-1-59017-498-2

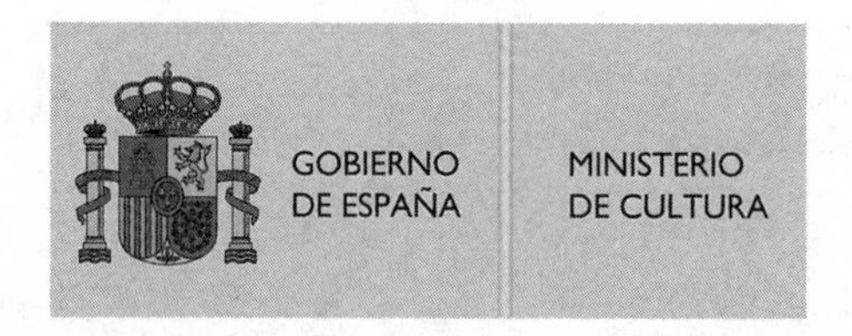

This work has been published with a subsidy from the Directorate General of Books, Archives, and Libraries of the Spanish Ministry of Culture

Printed in the United States of America on acid-free paper.
10 9 8 7 6 5 4 3 2 1

CONTENTS

INTRODUCTION

"TYRANNY is not a matter of minor theft and violence, but of wholesale plunder, sacred and profane, private or public," says Socrates to his listeners in the ninth book of *Republic*. "And yet, the real tyrant is enslaved to cringings and servitudes beyond compare, a flatterer of the basest men, and so far from finding even the least satisfaction for his desires, he is in need of most things, and is truly a poor man, as is apparent if one knows how to observe a soul. Throughout his life he teems with terrors and is full of convulsions and pains; in fact he resembles the condition of the city which he rules, and is like it." And he concludes: "There is no city more wretched than that which a tyrant rules."

Though Socrates's tyrant is a universal species, alive in every age and every country, Latin America seems to have been particularly propitious to his development (Africa in recent times and the Soviet bloc before the fall of the Berlin Wall are close contenders). Why one particular and vast chunk of the earth should display, over barely two centuries, such a catalogue of infamy is perhaps an unanswerable question. In a letter written in 1830, the liberator Simon Bolívar foresaw this state of affairs but did not explain it. "America [Bolívar gave Latin America the name of the entire continent] is ungovernable for us. Those who serve the revolution plow the sea. The only thing to do in America is to emigrate. This country will infallibly fall into the hands of an unbridled crowd of petty tyrants almost too small to notice and of all colors and races."

The fulfillment of his prophecy allowed Carlos Fuentes, less than a century and a half later, to suggest to his Latin American writer friends that they should each write a novel about their national tyrant and call the series "The Fathers of the Homeland." Fuentes realized that each of the twenty-seven countries of Latin America could boast (if that is the right word) of at least one tyrant; several had the pick of two or more. The project, unfortunately, never came to be realized, though it produced several other masterpieces: in Colombia, Gabriel García Márquez's *The Autumn of the Patriarch*; in Guatemala, Miguel Ángel Asturias's *El Señor Presidente*; in Paraguay, Augusto Roa Bastos's *I, the Supreme*; in Peru (though set in the Dominican Republic) Mario Vargas Llosa's *The Feast of the Goat*. Fuentes himself had published, in 1962, the now classic *The Death of Artemio Cruz*. To all five Socrates's definition can be applied.

The murky figure of the Latin American tyrant attracted writers from Europe as well. Beginning perhaps with Joseph Conrad's *Nostromo*, and continuing with Herbert Read's *The Green Child*, Graham Greene's *The Honorary Consul*, and, more recently, Daniel Pennac's *The Dictator and the Hammock*, European writers have seen perhaps in the tyrants across the sea foreign versions of others closer to home. Among them, perhaps the most complex, the most puzzling is *Tyrant Banderas* by Ramón del Valle-Inclán.

Born in one of the poorest districts of rural Galicia in 1866, Valle-Inclán managed to enter the University of Santiago de Compostela and, after graduating, began work as a journalist in Madrid. Under the influence of the modernist poets (notably Rubén Darío, then living in Spain), his first publications were, as one critic called them, "lyrical effluvia," describing a world made for human enjoyment, subject to human will, in which the hero is the soldier-lover, a cross between Nietzsche's Superman and Tirso de Molina's Don Juan. It was perhaps during his 1916 journey to France as a war correspondent for *El Imparcial* that Valle-Inclán radically changed his views on war and the uses of violence. From conservative aristocratic sympathies (he had presented himself as a right-wing candidate for the Cortes, the people's chamber, in 1910, and failed), the fifty-year-old writer switched his allegiance to the left (again he presented himself as a candidate, this time for the other side, and failed again). To depict the world as he now saw it, Valle-Inclán developed instead a harsh and unadorned prose in which he wrote his best-known plays and novels. He called these pieces *esperpentos*, that is to say, "grotesque and horrible things," the deformed reflection of the classic motifs of European literature. The first of his *esperpento* novels (and the best) was *Tyrant Banderas*.

Tyrant Banderas is set in the imaginary Latin American country of Santa Fe de Tierra Firme, inspired by Valle-Inclán's experience of Mexico, which he visited first in 1892 as a thirty-four-year-old incipient writer, and then again in 1921 as a recognized author. After suffering censorship under the dictatorship of Primo de Rivera, who ruled Spain from 1923 to 1930 (Valle-Inclán was briefly imprisoned for his anti-Rivera opinions), he decided to transfer his depiction of Rivera's tyranny to the wilder Mexican landscapes he had known, in part to use elements of the dictatorship of Porfirio Díaz in Mexico, in part to feel free from documentary constraints when speaking about his homeland. Not only Primo de Rivera and Porfirio Díaz served to create the character of Santos Banderas. In a letter to the scholar Alfonso Reyes, Valle-Inclán explained that it was "a novel about a tyrant with traits borrowed from Dr. Francia, Rosas, Melgarejo, López, Porfirio," all Latin American dictators. In any case, whatever his sources, the experiment was immensely successful. "What I've written before *Tyrant Banderas* is fiddle music," Valle-Inclán confessed in an interview. "This novel is my first one. My work starts now." He was by then sixty years old.

Tyrant Banderas is made out of fragments, snatches of dialogue, short scenes of action, but the patchwork effect is framed by a mathematically tight structure. Like Dante's *Commedia* (which Valle-Inclán read in his youth and greatly admired) the novel is constructed around the number three: seven sections divided into books, seven books in the case of the central section, three in each of the remaining six. The total number, including the prologue and the epiglogue, is twenty-seven (three times three times three). Furthermore, the story takes place over three days and is marked by three determining moments: the first in the prologue, the second halfway through the novel, the last in the third book of the third section.

This numerical insistence may be a reflection of Valle-Inclán's fascination with the occult in which the numbers seven and three carry a particularly numinous charge. His main characters are believed to possess superhuman powers. Tyrant himself is supposed to have a pact with the devil: he never sleeps, he has no intimate friends, he seems capable of the most incredible deeds. His opposition, Don Roque Cepeda, is also touched with a mysterious aura, but in his case his "occult" leanings come from his studies in theosophy, the ancient system of belief according to which the "seeker" was able to discover the working of all things visible and invisible, and communicate with ghosts. The entire atmosphere of the novel is imbued with a sense of the fantastic. Though nothing of this is made explicit, the uncanny, the otherworldly is constantly hinted at in local superstitions, in the commentaries of the indigenous people, in the depiction of the landscape itself.

Though the main characters detach themselves from the narrative as complex, many-faceted beings, it is the swarming crowds around them that are most powerfully present in the novel. Soldiers, natives, prostitutes, servants, prisoners, peasants, diplomats, and politicians constitute an organic monster ever-present in the narrative. In a multitude of tongues and for a large variety of reasons, this kaleidoscopic mass is the real protagonist of *Tyrant Banderas.* And like Socrates's tyrant, Santos Banderas resembles it in all its many ancient vices and perverted virtues.

To translate *Tyrant Banderas* is a task that seems impossible. To render the different tones and social strata of one language into another is difficult enough, so as not to have, for instance, Dickens's cockneys or Mark Twain's southerners sound, when translated into Spanish, like truants from Madrid or ruffians from Andalusia. But in the case of *Tyrant Banderas,* which interweaves not only many strands of Castilian Spanish but also various native tongues of Latin America, especially from the local dialects of Mexico, the difficulties seem insurmountable. *Tyrant Banderas* is not easy to read, even for a native Spanish speaker: most Spanish editions carry a glossary that is anything from seventeen to twenty-five pages long. However, proof of Valle-Inclán's narrative genius is that a reader in the original does not need to refer to the glossary constantly. After a few pages, the context lends meaning to the unknown terms, the gist of the dialogue is understood, names of plants and animals become recognizable in a landscape of words brought to life through the sheer vigor of the telling.

It is this driving verbal force that not only carries the action forward but also fuels the characters. As the narrative progresses, the mass of minor figures multiplies and coheres, and acquires the quality of a Greek chorus, punctuating and commenting on the action, while the individual characters grow in tragic force and become archetypal, larger than life. The second-to-last paragraph of the novel, in which the soul of Tyrant is finally laid bare (the reader must earn the horrific thrill of reading it), is one of the great moments of Spanish drama. It alone would serve to call Valle-Inclán the most important Spanish writer of the first half of the twentieth century.

—Alberto Manguel

TYRANT BANDERAS

PROLOGUE

I

THAT NIGHT the Creole rancher Filomeno Cuevas had armed his peons with rifles stashed by a jungle creek. Now Indians of the glebe advanced through Ticomaipú's murky swamps. A bright moon and whispering horizons echoing deep into the night.

II

The boss reached Jarote Quemado with a posse of henchmen, reined in his steed, and called the roll by lantern light.

"Manuel Romero."

"Here!"

"Step forward. My advice to you is go easy on the grog. The first stroke of twelve is the sign. Many lives are in your hands. Enough said. Shake!"

"Boss, we were born to this kind of bellyache."

The boss studied his list. "Benito San Juan."

"Here!"

"Old China gave you your orders?"

"Old China said gallop hosses into the fairground and turn everything upside down. Blast bullets and kill any dummies in sight. No big deal."

"On the stroke of twelve!"

"On the dot of midnight! I'll be there under the cathedral clock."

"Stealthy as can be. Remember to conduct yourselves like peaceful fairgoers up to the very last minute."

"That'll be us to a tee."

"Then play it like that. Shake!"

And the boss placed his piece of paper under the cone of lamplight, straining his eyes. "Atilio Palmieri."

"Here!"

Atilio Palmieri was a cousin of the rancher's wife—a fair-haired, stocky, cocky fellow. The rancher tugged his goatee. "Atilio, I've got a high-profile mission for you."

"Heartfelt thanks, cousin."

"Figure out a way to set fire to the nunnery, herd the nuns in their nightgowns out into the street, and cause total mayhem. That's your mission. If a nun catches your eye, look the other way. Keep your men off the hard stuff. Be ruthless, but keep cool. Good luck, Atilio. The last stroke of midnight is your signal."

"Count on me, Filomeno. I'll take this *avante*."

"I hope so. Zacarías San José."

"Here!"

"For you, nothing special. I mean, it's up to you. Say you and a few men pitch into Santa Fe tonight: Where do you think you'd hit the jackpot?"

"Give me one good man and there'll be chaos in the fairground. I'll bowl over the tent with the menagerie and fling open the wild animals' cages. What do you reckon, boss? Wouldn't that be a hoot? Give me five brave souls and I'll set fire to all the whiteys' stores. Give me twenty-five and I'll take out the praetorian guard."

"Is that the best you can do?"

"That, and I'll bleed Tyrant Banderas dry, too. Boss, I'm carrying the bits and pieces of my kid in this saddlebag. Out in the swamp the pigs chewed him up! But with him in this bag, I won big at cards, bought me a hoss, and dragged whitey through the streets behind me on a rope, before dodging the gendarmes' bullets. They didn't even touch me. Tonight everything's gonna be all right."

"Scarface, take as many men as you need and raise Cain. Shake!

But tomorrow morning, bury those remains. That sort of thing doesn't make you lucky in war. Energy and intelligence win the day. Now shake!"

"Boss, this fair will go down in history!"

"That's what I think. Crisanto Roa."

"Here!"

Roa was the last on the list. Now the boss blew out his lamp. Again the Indians marched in the moonlight.

III

Little Colonel de la Gándara, a deserter from the *federales*, jeered at the rancher's military pretensions. "Filomeno, don't be a fathead and try to leap over canyons when you don't have the legs! Your big problem is not to lead your Indians straight to slaughter. You hold forth like a general but you can't even read a battle map! Well, I can, plus I have a military school diploma. Common sense dictates that I should command, right? Is your stubbornness pride—or stupidity?"

"Dear Domiciano, war is not a textbook affair. You must be born to it."

"So you're predestined to be the next Napoleon?"

"Perhaps!"

"Filomeno, don't be such a fool!"

"Domiciano, draw up a plan of attack that's better than mine, and I'll put you in charge. What would you do with two hundred rifles?"

"Keep adding to them until I had an army."

"And how would do you do that?"

"By levying men from the mountain villages. The revolution has few friends down in Tierra Caliente."

"So that's your plan?"

"Yes, more or less. The game board for the campaign must be the sierra. The plains are for big troop movements, but guerrillas and other light forces work best in mountainous terrain. That's military science: ever since wars have been fought, the lay of the land has determined tactics. Two hundred rifles on the plain would be madness."

"So you'd advise us to pull back to the mountains?"

"That's what I said. Find a natural fortress that'll compensate for your lack of men."

"I like it! That's military science, that's what's taught in the schools! I grant you that. But I'm not a scientist and I've never seen the inside of cadet school. Domiciano, your battle plan's no good at all. As you must have figured out, I'm launching a coup in Santa Fe tonight. I've been planning it for months, and now there just happens to be a packet unloading at the wharfs that my men and I will be taking to Snake Point. We'll come ashore on the beach there. We'll take the prison guard by surprise, arm the prisoners, and incite the troops in the garrison to revolt. I've already won over the sergeants. That's *my* plan, Domiciano."

"You're staking everything on a single card! But what about Fabius Maximus? Do you think you know better than him? What's your plan of retreat? Have you forgotten a good general is never rash, never rushed, never attacks without a plan of retreat? That's what Fabius Maximus says. That's basic. I'm telling you, the general who grasps the burning brand and fights on our plains by skillfully abandoning territory, he'll defeat all the Hannibals and Napoleons in the world. Filomeno, revolutionaries have no choice but to play the gambit the Romans used against the Carthaginians. That's how it is!"

"Such eloquence!"

"It's irresponsible of you to lead a bunch of men to slaughter."

"Boldness and Lady Luck win campaigns, not algebra from the academies. How did the heroes of independence go about it?"

"On a wing and a prayer. They were popular myths, not great strategists. The leader of the pack was Simón Bolívar, and he was the worst general. War is about scientific technique, and you're transforming it into the spin of a roulette wheel."

"Too true."

"You're arguing like a fool."

"Maybe! I'm no scientist. I just follow my hunches. I'm off to Santa Fe to collect the head of Generalito Banderas!"

"Or lose your own..."

"We'll see. Time will tell."

"Yours is a campaign without tactics, banditry flying in the face of military science. Listen to the general staff of the Revolutionary Army, be a tiny grain of sand on the mountain—that's what you should do. But you ignore discipline and indulge in this fantastical foray. You're arrogant. You're ambitious. That's what you are. Pay no attention to me. Do what you think best. Sacrifice your peons. They've sweated for you. Now take their blood. Even-steven!"

"My conscience is clear. You won't budge me. My hunch will win the day."

"Your hunch is just a lust for power."

"You don't get it, Domiciano. I'll win this war as easily as snuffing out a candle."

"But if you don't, you'll have let your friends down and left everyone in despair!"

"*Or* serve as an inspiration."

"Yes, a hundred years from now, children will study you in the nation's schools! But now isn't History. Now we need realistic goals. All this talk is making me thirsty. Pass me your canteen."

He took a swig, struck his flint, and lit a dead butt, flicking ash over his Tibetan-god potbelly.

IV

The boss marched a mere fifty men through the mangrove swamp until he saw the packet unloading at a sawmill wharf. Filomeno told the pilot to throw the sails to the wind and heave to at Snake Point. The luminous reel from a lighthouse whirled on the horizon. Once the men had boarded, the packet silently weighed anchor. The moon navigated over the still life to port, a sailing ship on the beautiful briny. Its prow spurted sprays of silver and a black singer standing in the shadow of the jib drew a circle of listeners, declaiming poetry in a lyrical stream of liquid lisps. Sprawled on bunks, his students dealt out cards and oil lamps picked out sharp tricks by the hatchways and orlop decks. From the shadow of the jib the black professor continued to regale them with his lyrical, lisping bouquet:

> Thail on, swifth keel!
> Fear thee not!
> No enemy vethell,
> no thempest, no lull,
> shall make thee yield
> or thwerve from thy path.

PART ONE

A Symphony from the Tropics

BOOK ONE

Icon of a Tyrant

I

SANTA Fe de Tierra Firme—sand dunes, agaves, mangroves, prickly pears—Snake Point on maps of old.

II

On a hilltop, between pomegranate and palm, surveying the vast ocean and setting sun, the tiled colonial domes of Saint-Martin of the Mostenses were ablaze. A sentinel hoisted his shining bayonet in the belfry without bells. In those times of change, Saint-Martin of the Mostenses, a monastery from which the monks had been cast out by a long-ago revolution, served as the headquarters of President Don Santos Banderas: Kid Santos; Tyrant Banderas.

III

The generalito had just ridden up with his Indian battalions, after he'd executed the insurgents of Zamalpoa. Taciturn, stiff, silhouetted at a far window, watching the changing of the guards across the dingy grounds of the monastery, he looked like a death's-head in black spectacles and clerical cravat. He had waged war against the Spanish in Peru and he still had the coca-chewing habit he'd picked up during that campaign. Green venomous drool forever flowed from the corners of his mouth. Like a sacred raven, vigilant and still in his distant window, he reviewed his Indian squadrons, melancholy in their cruel indifference to pain and death. *Chinitas* and camp followers hustled and bustled among the serried ranks, ferreted for a plug of tobacco amid the coins and crumbs in their pouches, or found a copper for the keeper of the harem. A brightly colored globe burnished the sky-blue turquoise as purple shadows invaded the monastery's barren grounds. Some of the troops, Comaltec Indians from the depths of the jungle, looked up. The Day of the Dead; All Saints' Day: Santa Fe was holding its famous fiestas. At that distant window Tyrant Banderas was the scrawled image of a night owl.

IV

Holding bayonets rising from black rifles, soldiers marched through the monkish baronial hall escorting an unkempt bum whose face dripped blood. On the right flank, leading the way, Major Abilio del Valle's saber sliced the air. The jet-black doodle of his mustache stood in violent contrast to his white teeth wolfishly clenching the chinstrap of his broad-brimmed, silver-ribboned sombrero.

"Halt!"

The squad stood to attention and peered up at the monastery windows. Two corporals stepped forward, cowhide lashes strapped sash-like under metal rings across their chests, and stripped off the filthy blanket covering the prisoner's flesh. Submissive, speechless, back stark naked in the sun, his coppery body slid into the hole, a yard deep as stipulated in the Ordinances for Military Punishment. The two corporals threw some earth in after him and trampled it down, burying him up to his quivering shanks. His naked torso, straggling hair, and fettered hands stuck, dark and dramatic, out of the hole: he rested his goatee on his chest and watched warily as the corporals unfurled their cowhide lashes. The drumbeat thudded and the whipping began, the classic barracks punishment: "One! Two! Three!"

The lousy bum didn't even moan once, just puked all over his manacled hands, the irons sunk in the hollows of his chest. Blood spurted from his sides and the corporals kept time to the beating of the drum: "Seven! Eight! Nine!"

V

Kid Santos left the window to welcome a delegation from the Spanish colony. They were all dolled up in their Sunday best: the grocer, the pawnbroker, the lecherous playboy, the loudmouth patriot, the quack doctor, the bullying journalist, and the rich man of ill repute, the whole lot lined up to bow to the taciturn, wizened mummy with green spittle trickling from the corners of his lips. Plump, grandiloquent, and rotund Don Celestino Galindo spoke up, greeting the glorious pacifier of Zamalpoa with flattering hyperboles. "The Spanish colony wishes to render homage to a distinguished patrician, a rare example of virtue and energy, who has been able to reestablish the rule of order by inflicting exemplary punishment upon revolutionary demagogues. Nonetheless, in a spirit of noble generosity, the Spanish colony spares a prayer and a tear for those who have fallen victim to a deadly illusion, to a malevolent virus! But the Spanish colony must acknowledge that the only salvation of the orderly flourishing of the republic lies in the inflexible implementation of the law."

The row of whiteys mumbled their assent: some were rough, ruddy, and brutish; others had the jaundiced look of old shopkeepers; others, bejeweled and paunchy, were bursting with presumption. Their awkwardly gloved hands made them look like family. Tyrant Banderas spewed out a maestro's well-oiled patter: "I rejoice to see our racial brothers who are rooted here rising to the traditions of the mother country and affirming their unassailable faith in the ideals of order and progress. I rejoice greatly in the moral support of the Spanish colony. Santos Banderas is not the ruthless ruler his adversaries attack. Santos Banderas swears that the happiest day in his life will be the day he retires and, like Cincinnatus, returns to obscurity in order to cultivate his little plot. Believe me, my friends, the duties of the presidency weigh heavily on an old man's shoulders. A ruler must often stifle the dearest sentiments of his heart because the implementation of the letter of the law is the only way for him to safeguard hardworking, honest citizens. Tears may even well up in a ruler's eyes when the time comes to sign a death sentence, but his hand must not falter. This is a ruler's tragedy, and, as I said, it is more than the fortitude of an old man can bear. Among such loyal friends, I can reveal my frailties. I swear my heart was torn asunder when I signed the decree for the executions in Zamalpoa. I didn't sleep for three nights!"

"Oh, woe!"

The cluster of whiteys scattered. Their patent-leather bunions shuffled about the flagstones. Their clumsy gloved hands flapped hesitantly, unsure where to settle. The whiteys fingered their Brazilian watch chains in silent harmony. The mummy rubbed it in: "Three sleepless, starving days and nights!"

"Oh, woizme!"

Thus spoke a highland vintner from Santander, a squat, swarthy soul with a twang, with hair bristling like a hedgehog and a bull's neck that overflowed his celluloid collar; his shrill voice shrieked out at just the wrong time, like a theater claque. Tyrant Banderas took out his pouch and passed around some Virginian snout. "Well, as I was saying, my heart is broken and the responsibilities of government have become far too onerous. Find another man to sustain the nation's finances, to channel its vital energies. I am of the view that the republic possesses individuals who could rule far more successfully than this old veteran. Let the representatives of the nation and of the foreign powers convene to reach an agreement..."

He swayed his parchment head as he spoke, his eyes an enigma behind his greenish spectacles. And the cluster of whiteys cooed sycophantic dissent while Don Celestino cock-a-doodle-dooed: "A man of destiny can only be succeeded by the like!"

The line burst into applause, shuffling around the flagstones like steers swatting at hornets. Tyrant Banderas shook pompous whitey's hand as earnestly as a Quaker. "Stay on, Don Celes, and we'll have a game of slot-the-frog."

"It will be my pleasure!"

But as a parting shot Tyrant Banderas sent the other whiteys off with an aloof, curt farewell: "Friends, don't let me distract you any further from your important business. You have given me my orders."

VI

A barefoot, graying mulatto, breasts bobbling, brought in a tray of chocolate lemonade, the favorite tipple of friars and mayors in the days of the viceroyalty. Silverware and glasses tinkled in the maid's black hands as she glanced at her boss hesitantly, questioningly. Kid Santos grimaced like a death's-head in the direction of the trestle table that spread its spidery legs under an archway. The mulatto obeyed, flapping her skirts. Docile, moist, and lascivious, she fussed and slithered. Kid Santos wet his lips on the lemonade. "I've been drinking this cordial for fifty years. It's medicinal... I can't recommend it too highly, Don Celes."

Don Celes stuck out his paunch. "Absolutely, it's my favorite, too! We have similar tastes, and that's something I'm so proud of. I'm with you all the way!"

Peevishly dodging smoky spirals of adulation, Tyrant Banderas took shelter behind a taciturn snarl, the corners of his mouth spittle-green. "My friend Don Celes, silver bullets are what's needed to kill a revolution dead."

Whitey chimed in even louder: "Bullets that carry no gunpowder and make no racket!"

The mummy grimaced enigmatically. "That's right, my friend, silent ones are best. There are two critical moments in every revolution: the moment for drastic executions and the moment for silver bullets. My dear Don Celes, only silver bullets ensure the finest victories. It's politic now to make overtures to those in revolt. I respect my enemies and know only too well that they have many supporters in neighboring republics. There are men of learning among the revolutionaries, whose brains should be ticking on behalf of the fatherland. Intelligence deserves our respect, don't you agree, Don Celes?"

Don Celes flushed and smiled in greasy accord. "One hundred percent! I'm with you all the way!"

"I want silver bullets for those men of learning: they include some of our finest intellects. They outshine eminent figures abroad. Let them study in Europe and give us guidance from there. They belong in diplomatic circles... at scientific congresses... in committees for foreign relations."

The well-heeled paunch concurred. "That's what I call a sensible policy!"

And the generalito whispered confidentially, "Don Celes, I need a good supply of silver in order to pursue such a policy. What do you reckon, my friend? Be loyal, and let's keep this to ourselves. I'm taking you on as an adviser; I recognize how valuable you are."

Don Celes blew on his cream-frosted mustache, inhaling with sybaritic relish the barbershop aromas that rose up off his person. His large onion of a baldpate gleamed like a Buddha belly and his thoughts evaporated in a haze of Oriental mirages. "The contract for feeding the Liberation Army."

Tyrant Banderas shattered the spell. "You're giving this some thought, as you should. This is important business."

Whitey patted his paunch and exclaimed, "My wealth, needless to say, is nothing to speak of and currently much the worse for wear, but for what it's worth it is always at the service of the government. What help I can give is limited, but it represents the fruit of honest toil in a generous nation that I love like an adopted fatherland—"

Generalito Banderas interrupted, irritated, as if flicking off a horsefly. "Couldn't the Spanish colony stump up a loan?"

"The colony has suffered a lot recently. Nonetheless given its close links with the republic—"

The generalito pursed his lips and expatiated. "Doesn't the Spanish colony realize how the revolution endangers its interests? Then it should react accordingly. The government is counting on the colony to ensure the victory of the forces of order. Pernicious propaganda is plunging the country into anarchy."

Don Celes purred and swelled. "The Indian landowner is the utopian dream of university crackpots."

"Agreed. That's why I said that our men of learning must be given positions far away from the country, where their talents can do no harm. Don Celestino, ready silver is indispensable, and it's up to you to provide it. See the secretary of finance. Don't dawdle. Our accountant has the matter in hand and will put you in the picture; discuss guarantees and resolve everything forthwith. It's urgent to hit the revolutionaries with silver bullets. The news agency's slanders are seducing the foreign powers! We have protested these defamations through diplomatic channels, but that's hardly enough. My dear Don Celes, I leave it to your eloquent quill to draw up a statement that, signed by the preeminent members of the Spanish colony, will enlighten the government of the mother country. The colony must get these statesmen with their heads in the clouds to see that this revolutionary ideology is the yellow peril of Latin America. Revolution means ruination for the big Spanish landowners. They should be aware of that across the pond and act accordingly. Don Celestino, these are troubled times! I hear rumors that the diplomatic corps intends to protest the executions in Zamalpoa. Do you know if the minister for Spain will back such a protest?"

Rich whitey's baldpate flushed a deep red. "That would be a slap in the colony's face!"

"And do you think the minister for Spain has the nerve for that?"

"He's on the apathetic side . . . does what comes easiest. But he's not a straightforward fellow."

"Doesn't he do business?"

"He does debts, debts he doesn't pay. Is that big enough business for you? He views his posting to the republic as a form of exile."

"Do you suspect monkey business?"

"I do."

"Well, that must be avoided."

Whitey had a sudden stroke of inspiration and patted his bulging brow. "The colony can put pressure on the minister."

Don Santos's smile split his green Indian mask down the middle. "That's what I call slotting the frog's gob in one. You need to act urgently. The interests of the Spanish community run contrary to the utopian schemes of diplomats. All that equivocating over protocol shows they know nothing about the realities of the Americas. There's only one good policy around here, which is to view humanity as an entelechy with three heads: Creole, Indian, Negro. Three kinds of human. Anything else is pure idiocy."

Pompous baroque whitey held out his hand. "My admiration rises higher and higher as I listen to you!"

"Don't delay, Don Celes. In the meantime, I think I'll postpone my invitation to play slot-the-frog until tomorrow. You do like playing slot-the-frog, don't you? It's the medicine I take to relax and ever since I was a kid, my favorite game. I play every afternoon. It's very healthy and it doesn't bankrupt you like other games."

Rich whitey turned crimson. "Amazing how our tastes coincide!"

"Don Celes, see you later."

"'Later' being tomorrow?"

Don Santos swayed his head. "If earlier, earlier. I never sleep."

Don Celes fawned. "Master of Energy, as they say in our *Daily News*."

Tyrant bid him a ritual farewell, his voice slipping down a greased pole of cackle.

VII

Awesome as a bird of night, Tyrant Banderas loomed at the window. From that height he surveyed the open ground where Indian units armed with antique rifles maneuvered. The city shimmered in the reflected light of the emerald sea. A breeze wafted scents of orange and tamarind. Bright festive balloons lit up the distant, empty sky.

Santa Fe was staging its autumn fiestas, a tradition that dated back to the Spanish viceroys. Don Celes's fine horse and tilbury tripped lightly past the monastery chapel. A childish chessboard of flat pink and white roofs, the shining city climbed the hill above the harbor's curve. The white-capped waves glistened, and the barracks' buglers shot red flares into the deep blue of the desolate evening. Whitey's tilbury scurried like a black widow up the sunny end of the Mostenses slope.

VIII

A remote, motionless sentinel at the window, Tyrant Banderas continued to loom like some sacred fowl. The Mostenses slope floated in the seaside sunset's luminous glow and a blind man, pockmarked by smallpox, strummed his guitar. Prickly pears waved their arms like candelabra from Jerusalem. The singer's voice ripped through the misty silence of the sea:

> Diego Pedernales came
> from noble stock,
> but he didn't claim
> blood's privilege.

BOOK TWO

The Minister for Spain

I

FOR MANY years the Spanish legation had occupied a mansion with a tiled façade and gnarled timber balconies, next to a melancholy French pond that romantic tradition dubbed the Vicereine's Hand Mirror. With a high brow stuffed with licentious fantasies, the Baron of Benicarlés, His Catholic Majesty's plenipotentiary minister, radiated a morbid romanticism, like the vicereine gazing at her own features in her garden mirror. His Excellency Don Mariano Isabel Cristino Queralt y Roca de Togores, Baron of Benicarlés and Master Chevalier of Ronda, chattered like an old spinster and pranced like a prima donna. Bleary-eyed, stout, witless, and prattling, he exuded a saccharine sweetness. His hands and throat dripped flab; he parleyed with a French nasal twang; and his fleshy eyelids harbored gelid fantasies from perverse literature. He was a threadbare stuffed shirt, a literary snob, a dabbler in decadent salons redolent with the rites and catechisms of French poetasters. The shade of the ardent vicereine, taking refuge at the back of her erstwhile garden, eyed his love fests without women and cried her heart out, perplexed, jealous, and veiling her face.

II

All Saints' Day and the Day of the Dead. At such times the Vicereine's Way was full of stalls and sideshows, brightly lit and bustling.

Whitey's tilbury trotted foppishly until it came to a halt in front of the Spanish legation. A stooping Chinese flunky, pigtail dangling, was mopping the lobby. Don Celes walked up the broad staircase and traversed a gallery hung with shadowy paintings, carved wood, gilts, and silks: whitey experienced a hot flash of grandeur, felt pride and reverence welling up within him; the hum from sonorous, historic names buzzed in his ears and he quivered as if flags and cannons were on parade. His patriotic delusions picked up the rolling rhythms from strident, bombastic anthems. He halted at the back of the gallery. The silent, luminous door opening onto a long, deserted drawing room left baroque whitey curiously dumbfounded. His thoughts panicked and scattered like wild colts, rumps colliding. Suddenly all the Roman candles fizzled out. The plutocrat was irked to find himself in such straits. Stripped of emotion, bereft, terrified, as if he didn't have a penny to his name, he walked into the empty drawing room and muddied the gilded symmetry of its mirrors and consoles.

III

Sprawled on a chaise longue in a mandarin's kimono, the Baron of Benicarlés was meticulously delousing his lapdog. Don Celes walked into the room, struggling to re-create a conceited smirk between his protruding pate and ginger whiskers. His paunch seemed curiously depleted. "Minister, am I interrupting?"

"Come in, illustrious Don Celestino."

The lapdog yelped, and the diplomatic roué gawped and tweaked its ear. "Shush, Merlin! Don Celes, your visits are so few and far between that the first secretary no longer recognizes you."

A sly, stupid smile spread slowly and smarmily over the diplomatic roué's wearied, fleshy lips. Don Celes, however, was looking at Merlin. Merlin was showing Don Celes his teeth. His Catholic Majesty's minister remained aloof, evanescent, and equivocal as he eked out a smile with the incredible elasticity that neutral parties evince in times of war. Caught between the roué's grin and the lapdog's fangs and snout, Don Celes was as uncertain as a small child. He leaned over Merlin and oozed affection in a studied, sycophantic manner. "Can't we be friends?"

The lapdog yapped and settled back on the knees of his master, who was nodding off, his off-white eyes, faintly flecked with blue, bulging like two glass marbles, in an effort to match that product of polished deference and protocol—his fixed smile. A chubby, dimpled hand, the hand of an odalisque, patted the lapdog's fleece. "Be a good boy now, Merlin!"

"He's declared war on me!"

The world-weariness pervading the baron's puffy chops allowed his lapdog to slaver all over him. Turning a ruddier red between his ginger whiskers, Don Celes slowly reinflated his paunch, albeit with a hint of fear, cringing like a catcalled, tongue-tied comedian. As the petite lapdog simpered and slavered, the diplomatic nobody waffled nasally: "Where's Don Celeste been out wandering? What luminous opinions do you bring me from the Spanish colony? Are you not here as their ambassador? The way has been cleared for you, has it not, dear, illustrious Don Celes?"

Don Celes shrank back: ingratiating, acquiescent, resigned; the bulging temples, apoplectic flab, and burbling belly could hardly hide whitey's perplexity. He feigned a laugh. "Yet more evidence of your celebrated diplomatic wisdom, dear Baron."

Merlin yapped and the roué waved a threatening finger. "Don't interrupt, Merlin. Forgive his lack of courtesy and continue, illustrious Don Celes."

Don Celes tried to lift his spirits, prayed to himself, made a quick review of all the IOUs he'd issued to the baron, strove desperately not to deflate, closed his eyes. "The colony cannot afford to remain aloof from the politics of the country. They are central to its existence and integrity and the fruit of a considerable effort on its part. As a result of my pacific inclinations and a belief in liberalism when joined with a proper respect for government, I now find myself on the horns of a dilemma as I contemplate the idealism of the revolutionaries and the highly summary procedures of General Banderas.

But the Spanish colony has almost convinced me that Banderas is acting correctly. Don Santos Banderas remains the best guarantee of order there is. Victory for the revolution would be a disaster!"

"Victorious revolutionaries are quick to discover prudence."

"But it is right now that trade is in crisis. Business is bad, finances are shaky, bandits have returned to the countryside."

The minister rubbed it in: "And what's worse, civil war!"

"Civil war! Those of us who have resided in this country for many years see that as an endemic plague. But revolutionary ideas are a much more serious threat because they undermine the hallowed foundations of private property. Indian ownership of the land is a demagogic aberration that cannot possibly prevail in well-oiled brains. The colony is unanimous about that. I may have my reservations, but as a man who lives in the real world, I understand that Spanish capital has no choice but to oppose the spirit of revolution."

His Catholic Majesty's minister reclined on the chaise longue, clutching his lapdog to his shoulder. "Don Celes, is this ultimatum from the colony official?"

"Minister, it is not an ultimatum. The colony is only seeking to position itself."

"Or rather seeking to impose itself?"

"I have not explained myself well. As a businessman, I am unversed in shades of meaning, and if I have suggested in any way that I come in an official capacity, I have a special interest in rectifying the minister's impression."

With a glint of irony in his faded blue eyes, the Baron of Benicarlés sank his odalisque hands into his lapdog's silken fleece. He curled his flabby lips, still fatigued by recent indulgence, into a snarl of displeasure. "Illustrious Don Celestino, you are one of the most outstanding financial, intellectual, and social figures in the colony... Your opinions are indeed noteworthy... Nonetheless, you are not yet the Spanish minister. A truly unfortunate circumstance! But there is one way to remedy that: simply send a wire demanding that I be posted back to Europe. I'll endorse the request and sell you my furniture at a bargain price."

The rich man reveled in his clever repartee. "Including Merlin as an adviser?"

The diplomatic dolt greeted the witticism coldly and limply, simply killed it dead. "Don Celes, advise our Spaniards here to refrain from involving themselves in the politics of this country, to remain strictly neutral, and not, through any kind of intemperate response, to undermine the actions of the diplomatic corps. Forgive me, my distinguished friend, for not granting you more of my time, but I must dress in order to go and compare impressions with the English legation."

And the faded roué, in the waning light of his boudoir, fished his haughty blue blood for a suitably crushing gesture.

IV

Don Celes crossed the drawing room, his footsteps muffled by the carpet. More than ever, he was terrified that he was about to deflate. The ancient, pigtailed Chinese flunky was still mopping the flagstones like a manic child. Don Celes felt the complete contempt for the yellow man any whitey should. "Get out of my way, you bastard. Don't sully my patent-leather boots!"

The double shelves of his paunch swayed as he tiptoed to the door and summoned his swarthy driver. The driver was lounging in the shade of laurel trees with other down-and-outs, next to an outdoor bar. Skittles and piano rolls. "Get a move on, you idiot!"

V

The Vicereine's Way was lit up and bustling. Cheapjacks, guitars, gas lamps, bunting. Santa Fe was making merry, in a dizzy spin, in a feverish wave of light and shadow: Indian firewater and knives, cards and licentious dancing triggered violent, tumultuous images. The dark, desolate beat of life echoed across the open moat. In such a tragic, time-devouring frenzy, Santa Fe escaped from soporific, quotidian horrors. The festive din was as deafening as a war cry. Above crests of pomegranate and palm the tiles on the round colonial domes of Saint-Martin of the Mostenses shimmered in the gloaming.

BOOK THREE

Slot-the-Frog

I

HIS STINT at the office over, Tyrant Banderas walked under the archway of the lower cloister and into the Friars Garden. Hangers-on and aides-de-camp followed. "Duty done! Now, if you agree, my friends, let's spend the backside of the afternoon on an innocent game of slot-the-frog!"

He invited his coterie to join in, in that chummy, patronizing way he had, maintaining his vinegary puss and wiping his skull with a herb-scented handkerchief that was suitable for a schoolmaster or mendicant.

II

A geometrical ruin of cactuses and laurels, the Friars Garden enjoyed sea views: yellow lizards slithered over its tepid walls. The slot-the-frog board, with its fresh lick of green paint, provided the fulcrum for a twilight scene. This was the chosen entertainment of Tyrant's afternoons—his relief from tedium. Chewing coca leaves, he threw his quoit methodically and meticulously, and when he missed, his mouth grimaced a deep green. Keen to win, he never missed a move and was never distracted by the rounds of rifle fire that raised puffs of smoke along the sweep of the bay. Death sentences were carried out at sunset, and every evening a string of revolutionaries was executed. Oblivious to the gunfire, biliously cruel,

Tyrant Banderas aimed carefully at the frog's mouth. Puffs of smoke raced over the sea.

"Frog!"

Ever austere, turning his back on his coterie of cronies, he unfolded his handkerchief and wiped his baldpate. "Just watch me. Don't let anything distract you from the game!"

A sweet, pungent stench spoke of the jungle close by—where, come twilight, the stars burnt bright in jaguars' eyes.

III

Crouching in the shade of her lemonade and liquor stand, the old Indian slapped herself and smirked. Tyrant had given the signal: "Right away, boss!"

Doña Lupita clasped her Oriental, dwarfish hands together, pressed the ends of her shawl to her bosom, and pulled it over her matted hair. She smiled slavishly, a scheming serpent's sly glances, bare feet as smooth as her hands, words honeyed and deceitful. "I'm here to obey, my Generalito!"

Generalito Banderas folded his handkerchief with solemn scruple. "Earning money, Doña Lupita?"

"No, boss, learning to be patient! Patience and toil earn glory in Paradise! Last Friday I bought a rope to hang myself, but an angel intervened. Boss, I kept missing the hook!"

Tyrant Banderas painstakingly chewed his coca leaves, jaw quivering, Adam's apple leaping.

"Tell me what became of the manila?"

"It's tied to the Virgin of Lima, boss."

"What are you asking her for, dear?"

"That you, master, Kid Santos, should rule for a thousand years."

"Don't suck up to me, Doña Lupita! What year do your enchiladas date from?"

"They're just cooling down, boss!"

"And what else does your little stall have to offer?"

"Juicy coconuts. First-class maize liquor, boss! Firewater for gauchos."

"Ducky, ask this crowd what they fancy. The drinks are on me."

At the frog board Tyrant's toadies cowered before their mummy master. Twisting the end of her shawl, Doña Lupita demanded, "What would you boys like to drink? I can offer you the last three intact glasses I have. A drunken colonel smashed the rest to smithereens and ran off without paying a cent."

Tyrant pronounced laconically, "File an official complaint and justice will be done."

Doña Lupita twirled her shawl like a pantomime dame. "Generalito, you've got to pay just for the clerk to dip his pen into the ink!"

Tyrant's chin quivered. "That cannot be right. The poorest peasant in the republic is welcome in my audience chamber. Secretary Sóstenes Carrillo, establish a tribunal to investigate these grievous allegations..."

IV

Ruffling her skirts, Doña Lupe jumped up to fetch coconuts from the cool watered earth under her palm-frond shelter. Tyrant relaxed on the stone bench where the friars used to admire the view. His was a mind wearied by much woe. His waxen hands clasped the gold-topped stick with its professorial tassels, his chin shook, and his greenish mouth contorted into an equivocal, mocking, vinegary snarl. "Secretary, that young señorita there sure talks."

"Boss, she was just spinning a yarn."

"Typical filthy goat. The old whore! I've known her since I was a standard-bearer in the Seventh Light—almost fifty years. A camp follower."

Doña Lupita eavesdropped, shuffling around her hovel. The secretary addressed her with barbed wit: "Don't be scared, my dear!"

"I'll hold my peace, compadre."

"I'm not under orders to tighten the screw."

"O blessed judge!"

"So what military officer knocked your stall over, dear?"

"Kid, you put the squeeze on me and that guy will be back wanting revenge!"

"Don't wimp out. Tell!"

"Don't put the squeeze on, Secretary."

The secretary was happy sparring with the old woman for the entertainment of morbid Tyrant. With a pained look, Doña Lupe produced some coconuts and a machete. Major Abilio del Valle, who prided himself on how many heads he'd chopped off, requested the pleasure of putting the nuts to the blade: he did it as deftly as any Cuban *mambí*; a returning conquistador, he offered Tyrant the first nut like the skull of a hostile cacique. The old yellow mummy spread his hands and took the coconut half with an extraordinary show of thanks. "Dear Major, let that old moaner have the rest. If it's poisoned, the two of us will kick the bucket."

Keen-eyed Doña Lupe took the other half, toasting before drinking: "Dear Generalito, this old hide has nothing but respect for you: may Saint Peter and all the saints in heaven be my witnesses!"

In the shadow of foliage taciturn Tyrant Banderas hunched on the stone bench, an owlish black squiggle. There was something strange and scary about his shadow. His hollow, reedy voice sounded strangely imperious. "Doña Lupita, if you hold me in such high esteem, tell me the name of the drunken rascal who let himself go at your expense. Then you'll see how Santos Banderas esteems you. Give me your hand, my dear—"

"Big daddy, give it a kiss."

Without flinching, Tyrant Banderas heard the name the old woman whispered haltingly. Around the frog board his cronies fell silent, cowering and surreptitiously elbowing one another. The Indian mummy muttered, "Chop-chop!"

V

Tyrant Banderas left the board game like a rat on the prowl, cronies close behind. He turned into the cloister; the uniforms canned their horseplay. The mummy jerked his head at López de Salamanca, the chief of police. "When's the meeting of Democratic Youth scheduled for?"

"Ten o'clock."

"In the Harris Circus?"

"That's what the posters say."

"Who requested permission to hold the meeting?"

"Don Roque Cepeda."

"Were any objections raised?"

"None at all."

"Were my instructions carried out to the letter?"

"I believe so—"

"The propagation of political ideals, so long as it is within the law, is every citizen's right and deserves the full respect of the government."

Tyrant sneered. His chief of police, Colonel López de Salamanca, queried sardonically, "And, General, if there's trouble—do we suspend the act?"

"The Provision for the Maintenance of Public Order is undoubtedly clear on that front."

A smarmy nod. "President, sir, the firm application of the law will be my sole concern and top priority."

"Yes, and if you proceed with an excess of zeal, well, that is always extremely laudable, and it will hardly prove a sacrifice if subsequently you are obliged to tender your resignation. The government will naturally take your record of service into account."

Colonel: "Has the president any further orders?"

"Have you inquired as instructed into the vicious depravity of the honorable diplomatic corps?"

"Yes, I have, and I've made some sensational discoveries."

"I will be delighted to receive the information at the audience tonight."

The colonel saluted. "At your orders, General!"

The Indian mummy detained him further, grimacing greenly. "My policy is to respect the law. The gendarmes must assure order at the Harris Circus. Chop-chop! Tonight the Democratic Youth will set an example when it comes to exercising civic rights."

The chief of police quipped, "Civic and acrobatic."

Equivocal and sly, Tyrant's lips were fixed in a green grimace. "Well, who knows! Chop-chop!"

VI

Taciturn Tyrant Banderas walked on. As silent as at a funeral, his cronies trailed behind. He halted in the shadow of the monastery wall, beneath the watchful sentinel in the belfry without bells, bayonet slicing the moon. Tyrant Banderas stood and stared at the starry sky. He loved night. He loved the constellations: the arcane mystery of beautiful enigmas soothed his gloomy soul. He told time by the twinkling of the stars, wondering at their luminous mathematics and the eternal laws that governed them. The whole thing opened a religious vein within his stoic Indian cruelty. He went down to the lower cloisters and heard the nighttime cry of the sentinel in his tower. The ranks of the praetorian guard opened before him, presenting arms. Tyrant Banderas walked past, glancing suspiciously at every soldier's swarthy face.

PART TWO

Bellyaches and Fracas

BOOK ONE

Iberian Quartz

I

OFF-COLOR reds and yellows draped the balconies of the Spanish casino. Don Celes's rickety tilbury was waiting grumpily by the luminous edge of the terrace.

II

"Kill all whiteys!"

"Kill 'em!"

The diaphanous dome of the Harris Circus tent stood out against a green sky glittering with evening stars. In the flickering arc lights, raucous plebs crammed up against its doors. Pairs of cavalrymen stood guard in each side street and Tyrant's spies, embedded in the crowd, ferreted feverishly. Applause and hurrahs greeted the orators: they arrived in a huddle, surrounded by flag-waving students. Pale, histrionic, and heroic, they welcomed the multitude with a wave of their hats. The tumultuous tide, under the legislating truncheons of the gendarmes, opened a corridor to the Harris Circus entrance. Lights inside shone through the dark canvas dome. Flags waved. Roman candles exploded. People kept shouting and clapping, riotous and defiant in front of the Spanish casino.

"Long live Don Roque Cepeda!"

"Long live the Indians' liberator!"

"Long live . . . !"
"Death to tyranny!"
"Death to . . . !"
"Death to whiteys!"
"Death to . . . !"

III

Flower arrangements, gilded lamps, and rococo moldings. Big talk, strident, resonant, rough. The Spanish casino was lit up. The executive committee was closing a short meeting by arriving at a series of unwritten agreements in spite of boisterous rumblings of discontent in the lounges. A plot was afoot: rush out in a phalanx, break up the meeting with staves. Whitey's brass band blasted patriotic airs; bald bridge players slapped down stakes on the beige; uncouth domino players clattered their dominoes and bottles of soda; pool players emerged on the balconies to flourish their cues. Tartuffish grocers and pawnbrokers called for prudence and a squad of gendarmes to keep order. The lights and din brought a politicking, barrack-yard hum to over-ornate saloons that emulate the ministerial suites of the mother country: suddenly a phalanx of whiteys swarmed over the balconies. Screams of applause.

"Long live Spain!"
"Long live General Banderas!"
"Long live the Latin race!"
"Long live the General, Our President!"
"Long live Don Pelayo, the Moor-slayer!"
"Long live the Virgin of Saragossa!"
"Long live Don Isaac Peral, inventor of the submarine!"
"Long live honest traders!"
"Long live the Hero of Zamalpoa!"

Down in the street, the cavalry charged the swarthy, poncho-clad mob and the mob fled, machetes close to its chests.

IV

Protected by the gendarmes, bumptious whiteys spread out in the café. Defiant, arrogant, clapping. Don Celes was chewing on a long Havana between two of his sort: Mr. Contum, a Yankee adventurer with mining interests; and a Spanish landowner, renowned for his wealth, a dimwitted, dour fanatic from Álava, superstitiously devoted to the principle of authority that rules through terror and shock tactics—Don Teodosio del Araco, an Iberian rock of ages perpetuating the colonial tradition of indenture. Don Celes held forth with a self-made man's showy pride and an eloquence that was meant to dazzle the lackey pouring his coffee. Turmoil in the street as a melee of Indians bustled around the streetlamps. Town criers promoted the rally. Vinegary inquisitor Don Teodosio didn't mince words: "Just look at that rabble!"

Don Celes blushed and purred, "By authorizing such politicking the government of General Banderas is signaling its respect for all manner of political opinion. This action boosts his prestige! General Banderas doesn't fear dissent and permits open debate. Recall what he said when granting permission for tonight's rally to proceed: 'Citizens will see how the law allows the people a safe framework for the peaceful exercise of their rights.' Let us all agree that only a great leader speaks in that way. Personally, I think the president's words will go down in history."

Don Teodosio del Araco, laconic: "Deservedly."

Mr. Contum consulted his watch. "Yo muy interesado in hearing the spiches. So mañana yo am bien informado. Yo no oigo it from otros' lips. Yo oigo it con mis own ears."

Don Celes puffed himself up and delivered a great vacuous sigh. "No point in polluting ourselves in that stinky, poisonous den!"

"Yo muy interesado in hearing Don Roque Cepeda."

Don Teodosio expanded his bilious grimace. "A lunatic! An idiot! It's incredible that a man in his financial position sides with the revolution, people without a share to their name."

Don Celes riposted with pitying irony: "Roque Cepeda is an idealist."

"He should be locked up!"

"On the contrary. Set him free to get on with it. He'll soon bite the dust!"

Don Teodosio shook his head, rent by doubts. "You people don't realize that those preaching deviants have made the Indians restless. The Indian is naturally nasty—never grateful for the bounty he receives from his boss. He makes a big show of bowing and scraping, and he's sharpening his machete all the while. He's only reliable when under the lash: he's weaker, works less, and gets drunk more often than any Caribbean Negro. I've had Negroes, and I'll guarantee the superiority of the Negro over the Indians of these Pacific republics."

With gallows humor Mr. Contum pronounced, "If the Indio no so flojo, the white-skins would no vivir so safe in the Paradise of Snake Point."

Don Celes nodded, fanning himself with his Panama hat. "Too true! But your very formulation underlines how unsuited the Indian is to political activity."

Don Teodosio rose to the occasion. "The Indian is a lazy drunkard and needs to feel the white man's lash to work and serve society."

The Yankee with the mining interests interjected: "Mr. Araco, the amarillo peril can be very dangeroso in these republicas."

Don Celes protruded his patriotic paunch, tinkling the links of the great chain that girded his belly from one pocket to the other. "These republics will look to the mother country to ensure they never deviate from the path of civilization. It is from the mother country that these twenty nations seek illumination for their historical destinies!"

Mr. Contum's skinny, white parrot's profile stretched with scorn. "If the Spanish whiteys are still in control, it's thanks to nothing but U.S. guns and boats."

The Yankee half closed one eye and surveyed the curve of his nose. The Indians were still hustling and bustling under the streetlamps.

"Death to Uncle Sam!"

"Death to whiteys!"
"Death to all fucking gringos!"

V

At a nearby table, the editor of *The Spanish Criterion* was sipping a pineapple, soda, and kirsch cocktail that had brought fame to the barman of the Metropol Room. Pompous and rotund, Don Celes patrolled the pavement, fanning himself with his Panama hat. "Congratulations on your editorial! I completely agree with the line you take."

The owner-editor of *The Spanish Criterion* had an overblown, jingoistic, florid style and a fervid following among whitey grocers and pawnbrokers. Don Nicolás Díaz del Rivero, a prickly character, hid his hypocrisy under a coarse accent from the Ebro Valley. He'd been a Carlist in Spain, until he embezzled the funds of the Seventh Navarrese. In the colonies he lauded the cause of the restoration: he'd won two Great Crosses, the splendid title of count, and a bank on the basis of securities pledged, but nothing as an honest man. Don Celes swaggered over to him, Panama pressed to his paunch, taking his cigar from his lips and offering his hand. "What do you reckon about tonight's performance? Will we be reading your review in the morning?"

"Whatever the red pencil lets through. But please be seated, Don Celes. I have first-rate bloodhounds. One of them is bound to bring me whatever news there is. I hope we won't see any regrettable disturbance of public order tonight! All this revolutionary propaganda makes passions rise..."

Don Celes pulled up a rocking chair and flopped down, fanning himself continuously with his Panama. "If the rabble takes to the streets, I'd blame Don Roque de Cepeda. Have you seen that smart-ass lunatic? He could do with a spell in Santa Mónica."

The editor of *The Spanish Criterion* leaned over confidentially. With a grand, enigmatic gesture he calmed the tempest in the air.

"They must have set the rattrap already. What impression did you glean from your visit to the general?"

"The general is concerned by the attitude of the diplomatic corps. He means to abide by the law, which is why he has authorized this rally. Or perhaps, as you say, it's just a rattrap!"

"Don't you think that would be a masterstroke? But perhaps it's simply the concern you just noted... But look who's here, Larrañaga the Seer. Seer, come near..."

VI

Larrañaga the Seer was young and lean, pallid and smooth-cheeked: romantic hair, a loose bootlace tie, rings on his mournful hands, the sweet innocence of a passionate soul. He came over, nodding shyly. "Advocate Sánchez Ocaña has only just begun to speak—"

The publisher interrupted him. "Did you take notes? Pass them on. I'll take a look and send them on to the printer. What effect did he have on the audience?"

"On the masses—enormous. There was the occasional protest from the gods, but applause won the day. He had the audience eating out of his hands."

Don Celes looked up at the stars, as the smoke rose from his cigar. "Is Advocate Sánchez Ocaña really and truly such an eloquent orator? In the few dealings I've ever had with him, he's struck me as being quite mediocre."

The seer smiled shyly and avoided giving an opinion. Don Nicolás Díaz del Rivero directed the full glare from his spectacles at his copy. Larrañaga the Seer, hunched and silent, waited. The publisher looked up. "You lack political insight. We can't say that 'the audience greeted Advocate Sánchez Ocaña with a standing ovation.' You could write, on the other hand, 'Dutiful applause from a few of his friends couldn't hide the vagaries of an eloquence that was anything but Ciceronian.' You report in perfunctory fashion. You seem less and less a journalist every day!"

Larrañaga the Seer gave a shy smile. "And I was afraid I had overcensored myself!"

The publisher continued glancing over his copy. "'I found myself' is a gallicism."

The seer quickly corrected himself: "'I evidenced.'"

"Not allowed by the Academy."

The breeze brought a faint ripple of applause and hurrahs. The hollow voice of Don Celes boomed out: "Plebs everywhere are dazzled by metaphors."

The publisher looked reproachfully at his cub reporter.

"Why so much applause? Do you know who's speaking?"

"Probably the advocate still."

"So what are you doing here? Go back and help your colleague. Listen here, my little seer: I've got an idea, and if you pull it off it's going to be a prize scoop. Write the review like the review of a circus act, complete with tame parrots. Turn up the flimflam! Begin with a vote of thanks to the Harris Brothers Company."

Don Celes purred, "Now there's a pedigree reporter!"

Cryptically wrinkling his lips and lashes, the publisher ignored the compliment; he went on talking to the lean little seer: "Who's with you?"

"Friar Mocho."

"Don't let him be taken in by that crew!"

Larrañaga the Seer shrugged his shoulders. With a bored smile, he repeated, "See you soon."

Applause blew their way again.

VII

Touts shout on shiny pavements; Nubian bootblacks zigzag; waiters from American bars carry chinking trays aloft; curvaceous mulattoes conga by the side of the old dear in a shawl. Shapes, shadows, and lights proliferate and crisscross, multiplying hallucinatory, dark vibrations from the Orient ushered in by opium and marijuana.

BOOK TWO

The Harris Circus

I

BETWEEN dense foliage and beaming arc lights the Harris Circus spread out its dark diaphanous parasol. Gendarmes in pairs goose-stepped in front of its brightly lit doors; their drooping, strap-framed mustaches and jutting jawbones terrifying as Chinese masks. Crowds of ordinary people jostled wildly down the broad park paths: gangers with ponchos and machetes, Creoles in silvery broad-brimmed sombreros, villagers wrapped in cotton blankets, and Indians from the sierras. In the background, the diaphanous canvas with its metal lamps cut a triangle against the green sky and evening stars.

II

Like a drooping black buzzard, Larrañaga the Seer fluttered through the serried ranks of the gendarmes. The canvas dome vibrated with applause. Advocate Sánchez Ocaña was still singing his tenor aria. The little seer wiped his brow, untied his scarf, and sat down beside his colleague Friar Mocho: pockmarked and hook-nosed, an old salt of a scribbler who welcomed his companion with a vinous wheeze: "It's a speech and a half!"

"Taking notes?"

"You're kidding. It's a flood!"

"And it just goes on and on."
"For ages."

III

The orator dissolved a sugar lump in a glass of water, sipped, stuck out his chest, tugged at his starched cuffs.

"If the ancient Spanish colonies wish to return to the path of their historic destiny, they must listen to the voices of the original civilizations of America. Only in this way can we cease to be a spiritual colony of the old continent. Catholicism and its corrupt laws are the cornerstones of the whole civilizing, Latinizing mission in this America of ours. Catholicism and its corrupt laws are the fetters binding us to a discredited, selfish, and lying civilization. But if we reject abject servitude to religious laws, let it be to forge new bonds in which the ancient traditions of our millenary communism will be reborn, in a future full of human solidarity, a future that stirs the womb of the world with awesome, cataclysmic tremors."

"Your mother's womb!" a voice broke in.

Tumult: pushing, shoving, screaming, arms waving everywhere. The gendarmes dragged out a peasant with his head split open. Advocate Sánchez Ocaña turned pale. He smiled. With staged affectation, he stirred his glass of water with his spoon. The little seer muttered excitedly into Friar Mocho's ear, "If we could write freely! The boss wants merciless criticism..."

Friar Mocho extracted a little bottle from his shirtfront and bent down to kiss its neck. "Such eloquence!"

"Selling your conscience is shameful."

"Come off it! You don't sell your conscience. You sell your pen—not the same thing."

"For thirty miserable pesos!"

"It puts beans on your plate. You don't have to be a poet. Want a swig?"

"What is it?"

"Moonshine!"

"I don't fancy that!"

IV

The orator pulled at his cuffs, flashed his links, and approached the spotlights. A round of rapturous applause. He drew himself up like a tenor and resumed his aria: "The Creolocracy retains all the privileges and protections of ancient colonial law. The liberators failed to destroy them. Our indigenous people suffer the slavery of indentured labor just as in the worst days of the viceroyalty. This America of ours has gained its independence from Spanish tutelage but not from Spanish prejudice, sealed with the stamp of these Pharisees: the law and the Catholic Church. The liberators failed to redeem the insulted and defenseless Indian, working in mines and on landed estates, under the whip of the overseer. And our revolutionary faith, an ideal of justice inspired by human solidarity and stronger than patriotic feeling, is driven by the duty to redeem the Indian. The Pacific Ocean, the sea of our different peoples, hears the same fraternal cry of protest on all its far-flung shores. The yellow peoples have awakened, not for vengeance but to destroy the legalized tyranny of capitalism, the foundation of Europe's decrepit states. The tides of the Pacific Ocean rock to the rhythm of a unanimous outcry from Asia to the Americas. Still tossing in the nightmare they have endured for centuries, these people are gestating a new awareness, a new ideal, hewn from duty and hewn from sacrifice and mixed in an arduous, mystical crucible, one that will undoubtedly seem like Brahman lunacy to sordid Europe, besmirched with the concupiscence and egotism of private property. Born out of war and crime, the states of Europe feel no shame before their history. They boast of their crimes. They embrace their bloody rapine. Yes, across the centuries they trumpet their felonies and their cynical immorality. In schools youthful choirs are taught glorious anthems to degeneration. Inspired by our ideals, the critical spirit within these nations rejects the Roman and his doctrine of justice. That obese patrician, stooping over the cesspit, vomited the same creed. The owner of slaves defended his right to property. Spattered by the filth of greed and luxury, he made slavery the foundation of society and prospered accordingly: herds of slaves reaped the harvest; herds of slaves went down into the mines; herds of slaves rowed the triremes. Agriculture, the metal trade, maritime commerce couldn't exist without slaves, the patricians reasoned. And the master's brand on the slave's flesh became an ethical precept, inherent to the public good and the health of the empire.

"And we? We are not revolutionaries! We are not men who swear fealty only to the mean frontiers of the fatherland! No, we are the catechumens of a religious creed. Illumined by the light of a new awareness, we have come together here in the miserable confines of this tent, like the slaves in the catacombs, to create a universal fatherland. We want to convert the bare mountain of the world into a starry altar where everything that is worshipped is ordered by love. The worship of eternal harmony that can only be attained when equality reigns. Let us devote ourselves selflessly to our destiny as exemplary men. Beyond the crucible of misers and thieves, let us embrace a single desire—for that eternity in which our souls are cleansed of the egotism of 'mine' and 'thine.'"

V

Fresh tumult. A bullying gang of venomous whiteys bawled out from the arena.

"Hooligan!"

"Ignoramus!"

"Bankrupt!"

"Beggar!"

"Hoodlum!"

"Death to the revolutionary rabble!"

Whiteys, protected by gendarmes, screamed and clubbed. Tyrant's provocateurs wreaked havoc in the tiered benches. The two sides' competing insults came to a crescendo.

"Hooligans!"

"Death to tyranny!"

"Idiots!

"Bankrupts!"

"Beggars!"

"Hoodlums!"

"Idiots!"

"Anarchists!"

"Long live General Banderas!"

"Death to the revolutionary rabble!"

The Indians in their blankets on the terraces swayed in waves.

"Long live Don Roquito!"

"Long live the apostle!"

"Death to tyranny!"

"Death to foreigners!"

The gendarmes slashed with their sabers. Flashing blades, screams, hands held high, bloodied faces. The lights convulsed and blacked out. The big top collapsed. Sharp-angled canvas. Cubist vision of the Harris Circus.

BOOK THREE

The Ear of the Fox

I

SNIFFING like a snooping rat, Tyrant Banderas left the circle of sycophants and crossed the cloister. The chief of police, Colonel López de Salamanca, had just arrived, and Tyrant gestured at him to follow. The eternally nosey mummy walked through the locutory. The rest came behind, sidling along into the monastic cell where he usually met with his secret police. On the threshold he welcomed Don Celes as politely as an elderly Quaker. "Excuse me for a moment. Chief, sir, please come in and get your orders."

II

Chief, sir, strode across the room, winking and trading smut and spice in hushed tones. General Banderas was on the verge of entering the cell and stood with his back to them. Seeing that he might turn around at any moment, they all knew that they were in for a bit of a Punch-and-Judy show. Colonel López de Salamanca, chief of police, was just over thirty: a smart guy, silver-tongued, with a degree; the grandson of Spanish landowners, sentimentally and absurdly proud of his heritage and caste. The mestizo mob of Creole landowners, known as patricians in the republic, thrives on this inherited contempt for the Indian. The colonel went in, reassuming his mask. "At your orders, General."

Tyrant Banderas signaled him to leave the door open. Stayed silent. Then spoke deliberately, weighing every word: "This is what I want to know. Is the Democratic Youth out there done speechifying? Which parrots did the squawking?"

"Advocate Sánchez Ocaña kicked the event off. Set an ultrarevolutionary tone."

"What was it all about? Cut to the chase."

"Freedom for the Indians. Pre-Colombian communism. The 'Marseillaise' of the Pacific. Fraternity of the yellow races. Stuff and nonsense!"

"Any other parrots squawk?"

"No. There was a fracas between the whiteys and the locals, and the gendarmes had to intervene."

"Any arrests?"

"Don Roque and some others. They were taken to my office to ensure their safety."

"Quite right, too. Though their ideas are the opposite of ours, they are people of merit and their lives should be protected. If the rabble gets out of hand, lodge them in Santa Mónica. Don't be afraid of overdoing things. Tomorrow, if appropriate, I'll personally release them from prison and dish out sweet apologies. I repeat, don't be afraid to overdo things. And what news do we have of the honorable diplomatic corps? You remember what I said about Spain's illustrious minister? It would be useful to have some real evidence."

"An investigation was carried out this afternoon."

"How diligent! I congratulate you. And the upshot?"

"We've put that filthy bastard from Andalusia in the slammer—that rent boy-cum-torero they call Currito My-Cutie."

"What's the connection between him and the other character?"

"He's the pretty boy that slips in and out of the Spanish legation like a toy poodle. He has lurid press."

Tyrant drew back severely. "Not my kind of gossip. But go on."

"They arrested torero boy this afternoon on a charge of public disorder. His mannerisms were highly dubious, so we had his room searched."

"All right. Say no more. And the results?"

"The inventory's on this sheet of paper."

"Come closer to the chandelier and read it out."

The honorable colonel read with a church lady's twang: "A bundle of letters. Two signed photos. A walking stick with a monogrammed gold top. A monogrammed cigar case. A necklace, two bracelets. One curly blond wig and a black one. A box of beauty spots. Two ball gowns. Some silk underwear, garters."

Tyrant Banderas quivered like a Quaker and thundered his excommunication: "Repulsive abominations!"

III

The barred window opened onto moonstruck colonnades, where the black triangles of bats' shadows troubled the ruin's nocturnal whiteness. Dexterous honorable colonel took his time as he cheerfully shook jewels, photos, and letters out of various pockets. He lined them up on the table for Tyrant's perusal. "The letters are particularly interesting. A pathological case."

"Disgusting filth. Colonel, sir, put it all in the archive. The mother country deserves my best attention, and that's why I'm so very interested in protecting the reputation of the Baron of Benicarlés: you must promptly ensure the release of the slimeball from Andalusia. It would be most helpful if Spain's illustrious minister were to hear of this incident. He might even realize how ridiculous it is for him to be piping his fife to the tune of the English minister's folderols. Now what about the meeting of the diplomatic corps?"

"Postponed."

"I would be so sorry to see Spain's illustrious minister getting too involved!"

"He'll do the right thing, after that young chicken fills him in."

Tyrant Banderas nodded: lamplight glinted off his ivory skull and the round lenses of his spectacles. He checked his watch, a silver pocket watch he wound up with two keys. "Don Celes will throw light on the illustrious minister's thinking. Do you know, was he able to talk to him?"

"Yes, he was just filling me in."

"Colonel, sir, if you have no more pressing news, then let us bring this exchange to a close. I'm keen to hear the news that Don Celestino Galindo has for us. So please ask him to step inside and you stay here."

IV

Distinguished whitey Don Celes Galindo was fiddling with his walking stick and hat and looking at the door to the room: in the dim vestibule of the locutory his ridiculous rotundity made him look as petulant and self-preoccupied as an actor in the wings awaiting his cue. Seeing the honorable colonel peer out and about, he waved his stick and hat to catch his attention. His time had come, he sensed, and he swelled with pride at the earth-shaking role he was to play. With a mocking, commiserating glance all around, the honorable colonel summoned him: "Don Celeste, sir, if you would be so kind."

Tyrant welcomed Don Celeste in his usual rancid style. "So sorry to keep you waiting. I beg you to accept my apologies. I'm so keen to hear your news! Did you question the minister? Did you speak to him?"

Don Celes gave a look of disgust. "I saw Benicarlés. We debated the line the mother country should adopt toward the republic: there was no common ground."

The mummy's response was lordly: "I regret if there was friction—all the more so if I was in any way to blame."

Don Celes pursed his lips and shuttered an eye. The matter was trivial. "I have shared my impressions with a few stalwarts of the colony who have confirmed my conclusions."

"Tell me about His Excellency the minister for Spain. What are his diplomatic connections? Why does he behave in a way that is contrary to the interests of the Spanish colony? Does he fail to grasp that inciting the natives means ruin for landowners? The landowners will face the same stubborn agrarian problems he confronted in the old country. Legislators can't solve this sort of thing."

Don Celeste boomed out obsequiously: "Benicarlés is not one to embrace such a clear-sighted, acute analysis."

"How does he defend his position, I'd like to know?"

"He doesn't."

"Or his point of view?"

"He doesn't."

"He doesn't have *anything* to say for himself?"

"His position is that his views must not deviate from those of the diplomatic corps at large. I set out the objections and explained that it might lead to serious conflict with the colony. That he could be risking his career. All in vain! My words rebounded off his utter indifference, and he went on fondling his lapdog! I was furious!"

Tyrant weighed his words carefully as he spoke with mocking respect: "Don Celes, you must override your repugnance and speak to the minister once more: you must bring up the issues again, and make some very specific suggestions. You might try to explain to him the pernicious influence of the British representative. The honorable chief of police has evidence that our present difficulties are the result of an intrigue set in motion by the London Missionary Society. Isn't that so, Chief, sir?"

"Undoubtedly! The humanitarian pleading of those puritan proselytizers is just hot air—and a trick. The English always wave the Bible when they are bent on wrangling their way into our mines and financial affairs."

Don Celes nodded. "I am quite aware of that."

With clockwork precision the mummy leaned forward to redirect the conversation. "An honest Spaniard cannot bow out when good relations between the republic and the fatherland are at stake. Besides the gendarmes have provided an ugly new angle on the situation. Chief!"

The chief of police focused a mocking, lugubrious eye on Don

Celes. "The humanitarian principles of the diplomatic corps may have to bow before some stark realities."

The mummy: "And in the last instance, the Spanish colony's interests are not humanitarian. What's in the interest of the Spanish community is something entirely different. The minister must understand that! And give his support! If he's reluctant, inform him that that the gendarmes have evidence on file of his engaging in truly Roman orgies in which a prostrate pervert splays his legs pretending to give birth. Chief!

Don Celes was stunned; the honorable colonel launched his rocket: "Spain's illustrious minister apparently played the midwife."

Don Celes groaned. "I'm appalled!"

Tyrant Banderas scowled contemptuously. "Sometimes the mother country will send us maniacs."

Don Celes sighed. "I'll set up a meeting with the baron."

"Yes, and tell him that his good name depends on us. The minister will no doubt reconsider. Give him a most courteous greeting from Santos Banderas."

Stiff as a stick figure, Tyrant stooped. "Diplomats always drag their feet. Nothing will come of that first meeting. Let's see what tomorrow brings. The republic may perish through war, but it will never consent to foreign interference."

V

Tyrant Banderas walked into the cloister and bent over a campaign table. With a flourish he signed the edicts and sentences the secretary to the law courts, Carrillo, had just taken from a folder. Poorly painted martyrdoms, purgatories, sepulchers, and green devils glowered on the whitewashed walls. After ratifying the final document, Tyrant drew his Indian lips into their familiar green grimace as he drawled, "Chop-chop! Mr. Secretary, we're much indebted to the old camp follower of the Seventh Light. Justice demands he be given a good whipping. Punish him like a beggar! And he was one of my most invaluable friends! That idiot erstwhile companion of mine, 'Dainty' Domiciano de la Gándara! That buccaneer, soon to be dubbing me a despot, while winking at the insurgents! Punish him! Horsewhip him! He insulted that Indian camp follower and broke the pact we made and shook hands on. He's foul and slippery. Secretary Carrillo, what do you advise?"

"Boss, this is definitely a case of a Gordian knot."

Mouth still snarling and green, Tyrant turned to his chorus-in-waiting. "My friends, don't run off now: get a grip on the situation; weigh in. You heard what I was saying to our secretary? You know the fellow. A right-hand man. We all value him highly! If we beat him like a beggar, he'll be furious and join the ranks of the revolutionaries. So do we punish him and then release him, bursting with rancor? Should Tyrant Banderas—as the great unwashed call me—tread warily or magnanimously? Consider that my friends. I am interested to hear your conclusion. You are the jury. It is up to you—and your consciences—to decide the case."

He extended a three-piece telescope and leaned against a column of the arcade surrounding the hazy garden. He lost himself in heavenly contemplation.

VI

At the other end of the cloister his coterie ponders the pros and cons, exercised by the moral dilemma Tyrant has thrown them like a bone to a dog. Oily, foxy Secretary Carrillo tiptoes around the issue like a man of the bench. "What's the boss got in mind?"

Master Nacho Veguillas purses his lips. His eyes bulge and he croaks like a frog.

Major Abilio del Valle expresses contempt. He tugs his neatly trimmed goatee. "Your guitar's out of tune!"

"Dear Major del Valle, we will have to get our hands dirty!"

Secretary Carrillo harps on sweetly: "We have to guess what the boss is thinking and do that."

Nacho Veguillas played the fool in this farce. "Croak! Croak! I'll do whatever you say, Sec'cy my sweet."

Major del Valle muttered, "To get this right, we've all got to put ourselves in his situation."

"And once you have, my dear Major?"

"What, Mr. Secretary?"

"Give the crone the lie or beat Gándara like a beggar?"

Still tugging at his neatly trimmed goatee, Major Abilio del Valle flimflammed: "What I say is put 'Dainty' Domiciano up against a wall and whip him."

Master Nacho Veguillas had an attack of whimpering sentimentality. "But the boss might be swayed by old friendship. That spiritual bond could soften his severity."

Mr. Secretary Carrillo petulantly passed the baton. "Dear Major, dear Major, you must play Alexander to this Gordian knot."

Anguish spread over Master V's mien. "A squabble in a bottle shop doesn't warrant the death penalty! I reserve my verdict. I don't want Domiciano's ghost haunting me. You know what Pepe Valero acted in last night? *Fernando the Forewarned*. Boy! That's some episode from Spanish history!"

"That's a thing of the past."

"No, a fact of daily life, oh Major mine."

"Not to my knowledge."

"They go unpublished because the forewarned aren't crowned heads."

"The evil eye? I'm not a believer."

"I know an individual who lost at cards whenever he neglected to have a dead butt in hand."

Mr. Secretary Carrillo grinned broadly. "Well, let's get back to the business at hand. I suspect there's something else against Gándara. He's always been on the untrustworthy side, and recently he's been short of money. Maybe he tried to squeeze some dough out of the revolutionaries."

A whispering chorus of voices:

"It's no secret that he was plotting."

"Though he owes everything to the boss."

"Like every one of us."

"I'm the first to acknowledge that sacred debt."

"I couldn't repay Don Santos with anything less than my life."

"Domiciano's an evil ingrate."

They were in agreement. Del Valle passed his flask around.

VII

Skull lunar white, Tyrant scanned the sky with his telescope. "Five dates when the comet heralded by European astronomers will come into view. A heavenly event we'd be ignorant of if it weren't for sages abroad. In those starry spaces I expect they know nothing of our revolutions. We're quits. Nonetheless, Master Veguillas, our scientific backwardness is evident. You must draw up a decree endowing the School of Nautical and Astronomical Sciences with a good telescope."

Master Nacho Veguillas bobbed up and down self-importantly, stuck out his chest, and bellowed, "To nurture learning is to act patriotically!"

Tyrant greeted the poor cur's vinous elation with an amused nod of his skull, as his eyeglass revisited the night sky. Fireflies lit up the vague moonlit geometry of the garden with quadrilles of light.

VIII

Screaming, her hair straggling and her eyes beady as a mountain scavenger, a woman in a nightshirt swept into the room. Silence fell. All wrangling stopped. Tyrant Banderas recovered, swore, and stamped the ground. Terrified of punishment, the chambermaid and butler who had rushed after the nightshirted figure froze in the doorway. Tyrant thundered, "You fucker, is this how you keep her on a tether! You sonovabitch, you really kept a tight hold on her, didn't you!"

The two figures rocked in tandem on the doorstep and sighed—dark, hazy shapes shaking in the shadowy gloom. Tyrant Banderas went over to the nightshirted figure crouched in the corner, howling and frenziedly sinking her nails into her shaggy hair.

"Manolita, they'll look after you. Just go back to your bedroom."

The figure in the nightshirt with straggling hair was Tyrant Banderas's daughter: young, exuberant, burnished bronze, not much more than a girl, her enigmatic features set like a totem in a cruel frozen rictus of pain. Doubled over, she ran to take refuge in the arms of the chambermaid and butler, who were standing stock-still in the doorway. They marched her off, muttering dark threats, and disappeared into the blackness. Tyrant Banderas stalked up and down, caught in a stertorous monologue: finally he reached a decision. Stooped like a scarecrow, he climbed the stairs. "Major del Valle, arrest that bastard tonight."

PART THREE

A Night on the Tiles

BOOK ONE
The Green Boudoir

I

THOSE famous festivities on All Saints' Day and the Day of the Dead! The parade ground, Monotombo Square, and the Portuguese Mothers Arcade were crammed with liquor stalls and beer stands, roulette wheels and playing cards. The rabble rushes to see the toy bulls on fire being chased through the porticos on Penitents Way. Bands of jokers tear about snuffing out streetlights, making the flames on the bulls they're running burn even brighter. A buffoon, braggart moon dissects the vast dark sky: smoke from oil lamps blackens seedy entrances to freak shows, gambling dives, and hucksters' stalls. Blind men strum and sing to the huddled poor. The posse of Creole ranchers—ponchos, sabers, tall sombreros—takes up position behind the circle of gaming tables and fortune-tellers. Copper-skinned, barefoot, raggle-taggle gangs gallivant; on the church steps Indian potters sell clay bells covered with big garish circles and stripes. Hags in black and young kids do a roaring trade in funeral bells that tinkle gloomily like an Andean *quena*, recalling the legendary, suicidal Peruvian friar. Boisterous guffaws on all sides. In arcades and dive bars, guitars strum ballads about miracles and thieves:

> Diego Pedernales came
> from good stock.

II

Baby Roach's cathouse had strung colored lights across the square and lit candles for the dead in the Green Boudoir. Lupita *la Romántica* was in a hypnotic trance. In her crocheted wrap, her topknot at half-mast, she responded to Dr. Polish's excited gaze and gestures by panting, yielding, and, exhausted, emitting an erotic, "Ohhh!"

"Speak, Señorita Medium."

"Ohhh! In a dazzling light, climbing a broad staircase... I can't. He's gone... He's lost me."

"Go until you find him, Señorita."

"He's entering a doorway guarded by a sentinel."

"Does he speak to the sentinel?"

"Yes. I can't see him now. I can't... Ohhh!"

"Try to see where you are, Señorita Medium."

"I can't."

"I order you to."

"Ohhh!"

"Try to see where you are. What's around you?"

"Ohhh! Stars as big as moons shooting across the sky."

"Have you left the terrestrial level?"

"I don't know."

"Yes, you do. Answer. Where are you?"

"I am dead!"

"I shall bring you back to life, Señorita Medium!"

The mountebank put the stone from a ring on the sleeping strumpet's forehead, waved his hands over her, and blew on her eyelids.

"Ohhh!"

"Señorita Medium, you will now wake up, happy and without a headache. Very happy, wide awake and feeling no aches or pains."

He droned on, mumbling like a priest at mass. Big Mamma was shouting down the corridor, and in the square, full of dancing, drinking, and groping, Colonel "Dainty" Domiciano de la Gándara was having one hell of a time.

III

Colonel "Dainty" Domiciano de la Gándara twangs the strings of his guitar. Yawning gaps in his shirt and breeches coincide to bare the round, smiley belly of a Tibetan god. He sports slippers and wears a revolutionary *mambí*'s jaunty hat tilted to show off a red scarf and earring. Winking and strumming, he talks dirty to the babes in low-necked nightgowns, their hair hanging loose: big, black, with rippling muscles and curls, he's dressed in a sweat-soaked guayabera and baggy breeches held up by a belt with a silver buckle. Bacchanalian laughter bursts out after his every lewd joke. "Dainty" Domiciano, almost always in his cups, likes to hang out in dives and knocking shops, loves to raise the roof and make mayhem at the end of a night on the tiles. Unkempt and uppity, ladies of sin rock back and lap up the hustle-bustle from behind glowing red cigarettes. "Dainty" Domiciano spluttered, strummed, and twanged a last note of the most recent thunderous version of the ballad of Diego Pedernales. His brass rings glinted and his head shone against his gleaming guitar.

> The guards led the prisoner
> on a skinny steed,
> betrayed by an informer,
> in Valdivia's Field.
> A jealous farmer's daughter
> did the evil deed.

IV

He was tickling the sickly ivories in what they called the Green Boudoir Lounge. While the uproar continued out on the patio, the empty lounge loomed large and lit up, barred windows open to the marketplace, breeze rippling the muslin curtains. Blind Bright-

Eyes—his mocking moniker—played scales to the song of a skinny girl so depressed and ugly she looked like a workhouse slave. By the wall near the window two mulatto bitches vied over their fortunes as the cards were dealt: face paint brightened their sweet features and muddy honey complexions; their jet-black chignons bristled with combs—an Oriental drama in green tints and lacquer. Blind Bright-Eyes tickled the dirty ivories of the braying piano that passed its days in a shroud of black cloth. The girl sang, deadpan as a dead child, dragging the harmonies from her sad, swooping neckline, a small offertory tray gleaming mournfully on her chest.

> Don't kill me, treacherous dream!
> Your image in my thoughts
> is a bonfire of chaste passion!

In the pallid light of the empty lounge, her pallid voice struck an unbearably high pitch.

> is a bonfire of chaste passion!

Couples danced in the marketplace, swaying to the lilt of the *danzón*, languishing and lethargic, as they swept past barred windows cheek to cheek. Responding to the singer's tremolo, the colonel, lousier than a low-down bum, hit a chord on his guitar:

> Don't kill me, treacherous dream!

V

The green silk curtain balloons under the boudoir arch: a pretentious bed shimmers in the mirror. The altar candles flicker. Lupita moaned. "By all the souls in Purgatory, I've had enough! What a dream! My head's splitting!"

The mountebank soothed her. "You'll soon get over it!"

"Turtles'll grow beards before I let you hypnotize me again!"

Dr. Polish changed the subject, flattering the strumpet with his mountebank ploys. "You're a fascinating instance of metempsychosis. I'm sure I could get you a contract with a Berlin theater. You could be famous! This has been a fascinating experiment!"

The strumpet pressed her temples, stuck shiny, jeweled fingers into her dark tresses. "I'll have a splitting headache all night!"

"A cup of coffee will take care of that... Dissolve an ether capsule in your cup and soon you'll be back in shape, ready for another experiment."

"One's enough!"

"Wouldn't you like to try it in public? With clever direction, you'd be famous enough to perform in New York. I guarantee you a percentage. Before the year's out, you'll be framing diplomas from some of Europe's most prestigious universities. It was the colonel who told me about your case, which is of so much interest to science—from every perspective. You owe it to yourself to make a study of other individuals already initiated into the mysteries of magnetism."

"You're not going to dupe me again, not even with a wallet full of banknotes! That experiment almost killed me!"

"There's no risk when one adheres to scientific procedures."

"There's a rumor going around that the blonde who was once your assistant died on stage."

"That I was in prison? That's a bald-faced lie! Do I look like I'm in jail?"

"You must have filed the bars of your cell."

"You think I've got those kind of powers?"

"You're a wizard, aren't you?"

"The study of magnetic phenomena can in no way be described as wizardry. Are you now free of your cephalic discomfort?"

"Yes, it seems to be going away."

Big Mamma shouted down the passage, "Lupita, somebody wants you."

"Who?"

"A friend. Get a move on!"

"I'm off. If I wasn't so hard up, I'd have kept tonight free to worship Blessed Souls."

"Lupe, you could be big on stage."

"The very thought scares me stiff!"

She swept out of the boudoir, skirts rustling, followed by Dr. Polish. That necromantic rogue, with his fairground show, was in big demand at Baby Roach's cathouse.

BOOK TWO

Illumination from the Spirits

I

> He rode out with a town crier
> on a donkey from the court.
> He swore at the executioner,
> who slipped on the hood
> and flashed a Masonic finger
> at where Jesus stood.

THE NAKED sinners stopped whispering. They waited in the Green Boudoir by the oil lamps and candles on the altar. They heard the ballad and the strumming of the guitar. Moths whirred around the flames on the altar. Lovers muttered by the head of the bed.

Strumpet: "He was obscene!"

Pimp: "Atheist!"

"That song sounds blacker than the tomb tonight."

"Happy in life, sad in death!"

"Crap! You caw like a crow! At the final trump, Veguillas, will you confess like a Christian?"

"I've never denied the soul's eternal life!"

"Dear Nacho, we are Spirit as well as matter! This flesh of mine houses a romantic! If I weren't so hard up, I'd have observed All Saints'. But I'm up to my neck in debt to Madame! Nachito, who doesn't have their dead to honor? Orphans, yeah, but they just don't know who their dead are. This day should be the most honored day of all. It brings back so many memories! If you were a romantic, you'd do your duty. You'd pay my dues and leave."

"What if I left without paying?"

"Sure. That's how romantic I am! But I'm telling you that if I didn't owe Big Mamma—"

"You want me to close your account?"

"What are you getting at?"

"Do you want me to pay off your debt?"

"Don't pull my leg, Nachito."

"Do you owe a lot?"

"Thirty Manfreds! I gave her fifteen in the May Pole Festival! Since you took over my debt, I was going to be a loyal slave!"

"I'm no slave-keeper, sorry!"

The strumpet gazed wonderingly at her glittering fake rings. She thought back. Her painted mouth complained: "We've had this conversation. Don't you remember, Veguillas? Same words, yes, same big talk."

The sinner was lost in thought, entranced by the fake gems in her rings. Veguillas was just as lost.

II

They could hear guitars playing, singing, and hoots of laughter, clapping, and heel-tapping as the girls got into stride. Shouting, running, slamming doors. Panting and stamping in the passage. Knuckles cracking and Taracena bawling, "Bolt those doors! 'Dainty' Domiciano's after you with a song. Bolt them, if you ain't already. He's hell-bent on raising Cain in the bedrooms."

Still focused on her fabulous hands, the romantic heaved a sigh. "Domiciano knows how to live it up!"

"And when it's wake-up time?"

"Hail Mary! Haven't we had this conversation, Veguillas? What were you saying about the bad end in store for dear little Colonel de la Gándara?"

Veguillas blustered. "That secret never passed my lips!"

"I've got my doubts! I spied Old Nick in your eyes just then, Nachito!"

"Lupita, are you seeing things?"

He was coming up the passage; the din of his singing, strumming, clapping, and stamping grew louder. Their friend sang a song from the plains:

> Master Veguillas
> take your lady
> and raise a glass
> to the Spirits.

"Holy God! The same song they sung when we was in bed together!"

Half amused, half frightened, Nacho Veguillas gave her a ringing slap on her ass.

"Lupita, you're just too romantic!"

"Don't get me into a state, Veguillas!"

"You've been pulling my leg all night."

Song and guitar returned to the boudoir door. Candles and crosses shook on the altar. The girl muttered, "Nacho Veguillas, do you get along with 'Dainty' Domiciano?"

"Best friends!"

"Why don't you tip him off so he can save his skin?"

"What do you know?"

"Didn't we just talk about it?"

"We sure didn't!"

"You swear, Nachito?"

"I swear!"

"We said nothing? Well, it must have been on your mind!"

Nacho Veguillas jumped up, eyes popping out of their sockets. He stood on the rug, hands over his privates.

"Lupita, you do business with the Spirits!"

"Shush!"

"Tell me!"

"I'm so confused! You're saying we didn't say a thing about what's in store for Colonel de la Gándara?"

Someone banged on the door. The din resumed. Song and guitar:

> Get up, friend,
> put on your pants.
> so we can deal
> a few quick hands!

The little colonel kicked the door open and walked in. He strummed his guitar and it wobbled on his potbelly. Nacho Veguillas ran around crazy with joy. "Croak! Croak!" he sang, just like a frog.

III

Under the bright bunting of the fiesta, the cathouse's patio was a riot of liquor and cake. Tired hands of cards were dealt: they were so bad that the stakes on the beige in the lamp's yellow haze shrank to nothing. Money was getting scarce, so Taracena brought in sugarcane rum and maize beer to perk things up. There was a burst of applause as Nacho Veguillas, half naked, waistcoat unbuttoned, with his suspenders trailing behind him like a tail, hopped up and down and did the toad-and-frog duet, classical music that Tyrant Banderas loved to soothe his gloomy spirits with. Like a sobbing busker, Nacho greeted the hurrahs, shook hands, and reeled from epic embrace to epic embrace. Dr. Polish, jealous of Nacho's success, harangued a group of girls, waving his cards like a fan. The whores sat on the edges of their seats, sealed in a circle of pretty bows and bleary eyes, whispering tropical sweet nothings. The melancholy diva passed around a little offertory tray, stretching her sad swooping neck, pale and hangdog, horrid in a blue muslin bodice and hideously marked by hunger. Nachito hopped after her, making a great hoo-ha. "Croak! Croak!"

IV

Dawn broke and a drowsy couple, the blind owl and shrouded girl, drifted past the Portuguese Mothers Arcade. The bright lights of the fiesta were going out. A few stands still lined the arcade; the merry-go-round spun one final time. The blind owl and shrouded girl stumbled along, muttering darkly, “Never known times as bad as these!”

Looking like death warmed up, the girl spoke: “A fiesta used to be different!”

Owl shook his head. “Baby never brings in fresh women; that’s no way to run a business. What’s that girl from Panama like? Does she rake it in?”

“Not much—she’s *too* new. She’s crazy!”

“How come?”

“’Cuz of a girl they call the *malagueña*! She knows how to stir things up.”

“Don’t talk like those women.”

The shrouded girl stared up sadly at a star. “Was my voice very hoarse?”

“Only the first notes . . . Tonight you showed the passion of a true artist. If your father didn’t love you, you could be a huge success in concert halls. ‘Don’t kill me, treacherous dream.’ Divine! Dear daughter, you’ve got to start singing in concert halls so that I don’t have to live from hand to mouth anymore. I could conduct.”

“Blind?”

“After I got my cataracts removed!”

“Dear Father, you do like to dream!”

“Won’t we ever escape this nightmare?”

“Who knows?”

“You’ve got doubts?”

“I’m not saying a thing.”

“You’ve never known any other life—you’re resigned to your fate.”

“You, too, Daddy!”

"I know how other people live. I know how different things could be."

"You envy them? I don't envy the rich."

"So who do you envy?"

"A bird! Singing on the branch of a tree."

"You don't know what you're talking about."

"We're here."

An Indian and his woman were asleep under a blanket in the doorway. The funereal girl and owlish blind man wriggled past. The nuns' bell clanged for the dead.

V

Slurping wine over his lips and drinking deep of tender eyes, Nacho Veguillas rests his head on his strumpet's bosom and sings in the Green Boudoir, "Love me, my lily in the mud!"

The harlot swooned. "My cinnamon boy! And you say you aren't romantic!"

"Purest angel of love, my inspiration, my love! I'll save you from the abyss. I'll redeem your virgin soul! Taracena! Taracena!"

"Don't make such a racket, Nachito! Leave Madame alone. She's in no mood to hear your complaints."

The girl on the game covered his drunken mouth with her ringed fingers. Nachito sat up. "Taracena! I'll pay everything you owe to this lily trapped in the vile mud of your trade!"

"Shuddup! Don't set yourself up!"

Tears dripped from Nachito's cruet nose. He turned to the whore. "Slake my thirst for the ideal, angel with broken wings! Soothe my brow with your hand. My brain is burning in a lava sea!"

"Where have I heard music like that before? Those same words, Nachito, I heard them right here!"

Nachito was jealous. "Some asshole!"

"Or maybe not. Tonight it seems like everything's happened before. Must be the Blessed Spirits . . . ! Like everything happens before it really does!"

"In lonely dreams I called to you. Your gaze draws me like a magnet! Kiss me, my love!"

"Nachito, don't be so silly. Leave me alone to pray to the Spirits."

"Kiss me, Jarifa! Kiss me, shameless innocent! A chaste, virginal kiss! I was alone in the desert of life when an oasis of love appeared on the horizon where now I rest my brow!"

Nachito sobbed. The girl's lips were painted like a valentine. She pressed them against his—a sweet kiss right out of a novelette. "Ohhh, you're such a silly!"

VI

The altar of the Blessed Spirits quivered. Flickering reflections rent the walls of the Green Boudoir. The door opened and without ceremony little Colonel de la Gándara walked in. Veguillas turned his cruet nose with a doe-eyed look: "'Dainty' Domiciano, don't profane the idyll of two souls!"

"Master V, you need a dose of ammoniac. Look at me, free of the vapors. Guadalupe, why don't you splash some holy water on him?"

Colonel de la Gándara stamped around and the candles on the little altar went crazy, while the irreverent clatter of his silver spurs set up a heretical, symphonic accompaniment. The colonel had changed: his breeches were tucked into his riding boots, his belt was pulled tight, his machete hung at his side, his beard was freshly cut, and a shining black lock was combed down over his brow. "Veguillas, pal, lend me twenty sols. You cleaned up at the gaming table. I'll pay you back tomorrow."

"Tomorrow!"

The word vanishes into the room's green penumbra. Nachito stands and gapes. A distant bell chimes. The altar lights grow dim and trembly. The jet-black harlot in the pink shirt crossed herself behind the curtains. Little Colonel de la Gándara droned on. "Tomorrow. Or when I die!"

Nachito moaned. "Death is never far away. Domiciano, come to your senses. Money's not going to help."

The strumpet strutted out from behind the curtains, lacing her corset. Her breasts were naked. A pink garter pulled her nylon stockings tight. "Domiciano, save yourself! This jerk's not talking, but he knows you're on Tyrant Banderas's wanted list."

The colonel stared at Veguillas. Veguillas threw up his arms in shock. "Evil angel!" he shouted. "Bio-magnetic viper! Your intoxicating kisses sucked out my thoughts."

The colonel reached the door in a single leap. He was on the lookout, alert. He shut the door and locked it, planting his legs firmly apart and pulling out his machete. "Lupita, bring the basin. We'll bleed this doctor gratis."

The corseted strumpet pushed herself between the two men. "Take it easy, Domiciano. Before you get to him, you'll have to run me through. What were you trying to do? What's this all about? You're in danger? So—run for your life!"

Colonel de la Gándara tweaked his mustache contemptuously. "Who's betrayed me, Veguillas? What's the big threat? Tell me, or I'll turn over your passport to the Blessed Spirits. Come on!"

Cringing by the wall and feeling sorry for himself, Veguillas tried to pull on his trousers. His hands shook. He moaned in terror. "Buddy, the old camp follower with the little stall next to the frog game informed on you. It's her!"

"Bloody bitch!"

"If you didn't always like to get so drunk and pushy—"

"I'm going to flay the old bitch for a drum skin!"

"Kid Santos made a deal with her to give you a whipping."

The whore was insistent. "Domiciano, don't waste time!"

"Shut up, Lupita! This nice friend of yours is now going to tell me who's tried and convicted me."

Veguillas squirmed. "Domiciano, don't fuck up. It's not like you don't know how things work here."

VII

The little colonel waved his gleaming machete in the air. The whore, in her pink nightgown, shut her eyes tight and waved her arms. Veguillas, in his undershirt, was cringing by the wall with his pants in his hands. The colonel snatched them away. "Fuck your pants! What have they sentenced me to?"

Nachito shrunk up, his cruet nose grazing his navel. "Brother, stop asking questions! Every word is like a bullet... I'm committing suicide! If it's not you, it'll be me."

"But what is it? And who decided?"

The whore was in despair, kneeling before the candlelit altar. "Save your skin! If you don't go, Major del Valle will come and arrest you!"

Nachito was terrified. "Foul, foul hag!"

He curled up in a ball, his feet under the tail of his shirt. The colonel picked him up by his hair. Veguillas flailed wildly, his shirt yanked north of his navel. The colonel bellowed, "Is del Valle under orders to arrest me? Out with it."

Veguillas's tongue was hanging out. "I have committed suicide!"

BOOK THREE

A Touch of Guignol

I

IT WAS like a movie chase! As soon as the colonel hits the street he spots the rifles of the patrol advancing along the Portuguese Mothers Arcade: Major del Valle on the way to arrest him. Heart racing like mad, he drops to the ground and crawls across the street. A half-naked Indian with a bandaged chest cracks a door open. He slips through. Veguillas follows, sucked into the cycle of absurd coincidences. Stooped like a rider, the colonel dashes upstairs. Nachito, scrabbling behind, is dazzled by the glare of his spurs. Under the attic skylight the colonel waits outside a door, panting. A servant girl, with a broom, opens it. Arms flailing in panic, she sees the two fugitives hurl themselves into the corridor. She screams, then the sharp glint of a blade puts a brake on her tongue.

II

At the end of the passage a student's bedroom. A young man, pale from reading, pores over an open book, elbows on his desk. The lamp smokes. His window is open to the evening star. The colonel walks in, points. "What's out the window?"

Shaking with shock the student turns to the window. Without waiting for a reply, the colonel puts his legs over the sill. "Come on, you bastard!" he shouts mischievously.

Nachito is frantic. “Fuck your mother!”

“Whoopee!” the colonel yells and lets go.

He hurtles through the air. Falls on a small roof. Smashes roof tiles. Crawls away. Nachito peers out, tears dripping from his cruet nose, his face a mass of wrinkles. “O to be a cat!”

III

Major del Valle flashes his saber through the cathouse’s bedrooms. He races from room to room, followed by his soldiers, spurs flashing and tinkling: at his side Big Mamma buoys her buttocks, sighs, and ponders, a flower behind one ear and slippers on her feet. “Chief, I’m from Cadiz and I never lie! My word is as good as the king of Spain’s! Only a second ago Colonel Gandarita said, ‘I’m off!’ He came and went. Just now. It’s a miracle you didn’t run into him! He’d just gone three steps when your soldiers dashed through the door!”

“Didn’t he say where he was heading?”

“He shot out like a thunderbolt! If he’s not after booze, he’ll be looking for a bed.”

The major looked at the bawd and called to his sergeant, “Search the house. If I find smuggled goods, Baby Roach, it’ll be a hundred lashes.”

“Kid, you ain’t gonna find a thing.”

Big Mamma rattled her keys. The major tugged his goatee uneasily. He decided to go to the lounge to wait. In dawn’s ashen light, the cathouse was full of fear, screams, furtive dashes, rude ditties. Lupita loomed in the Green Boudoir’s arch, high-heeled, a new beauty spot on her cheek, cigarette smoke billowing from her lipstick valentine. “Abilio, I really like you!”

“I’m off.”

“Hey, do you still think Domiciano’s hiding here? Your rattrap missed him. Now you’ll have to send out the dogs!”

IV

And Nachito Veguillas is still standing by the student's window looking grim. Time seems frozen; every action hangs absurdly on the poised second, stupefied, crystallized, bright, unreal, like under marijuana. Awake, his hair a mess, the student looks on in astonishment from behind his books and desk. Nachito stands opposite, his mouth agape, his hands covering his ears. "I've committed suicide!"

The student looks more deathly by the moment. "Have you escaped from Santa Mónica?"

Nachito rubs his eyes. "This is all so crazy... My friend, I'm not running away from anyone. I'm just here. Take a look at me. I'm not on the run... I'm not guilty. I'm only in tow... If you want to know why I'm here, it's hard to know what to say. I don't even know where I am! I rushed up here on impulse, swept along by that other guy. Take my word. This whole thing is just too much. Bio-magnetism!"

The student is in a quandary, unable to decipher the nightmarish imbroglio he'd glimpsed on the glaring face of the guy who flung himself out the airy window that had stayed open all night, with the inertia of an inanimate object, waiting for that minute of low melodrama. Nachito sobs and whimpers uncontrollably. "So here I am, young sir. Please can I have a drop of water? I need to calm down. This must be a dream."

But the words stick in his craw. Voices and weapons clatter down the passage. Clutching a revolver, Major Abilio del Valle fills the doorway. Behind him soldiers point their rifles. "Hands up!"

V

Another door opens on a barefoot giantess in petticoat and scarf. Lion tresses. Jet-black eyes and brows that smolder like embers in her face. A mighty bulging-biceped Old Testament figure with the pathos of a baroque sculpture. And now she rushes in, Doña Rosita Pintado, a whirlwind of angry cries, gestures, scowls. "What are you doing in *my* house? Are you thinking of taking my boy? Who's in command here? Take me then! Is this what you call *legal*?"

Major del Valle spoke: "Don't make me laugh, Doña Rosita. This tender shoot needs to come and make a statement right away. I guarantee he'll be back once that's done—if he's not implicated. Don't be afraid. Under the circumstances, it's the least I can do. The boy will be back, at least if he's blameless, I promise."

The youngster glanced at his mother, scowling at her to shut up. The giantess quivered with misery and ran to hug him. Her son stopped her in her tracks. "Be quiet, Mamma. Don't put your foot in it. Arguing won't get us anywhere."

His mother brayed, "You'll be the death of me, you Guinean black!"

"I'll be safe enough!"

Stunned, the giantess sank down into a dark sea of doubt and alarm. "Major del Valle, what's this all about—!"

The boy broke in: "A fugitive from the law escaped through my window."

"And what did you say to him?"

"I didn't even see his face—"

Major del Valle interrupted. "All you have to do is say as much in the proper place and that will be that."

The giantess folded her arms. "Do we know who it was?"

Nachito spoke out of an alcoholic haze: "Colonel de la Gándara!"

Glistening with tears, cowering between two soldiers, Nachito shot snot from his dripping cruet. Bewildered and dismayed, Doña Rosita stared at him. "What are you crying about?"

"I've committed suicide!"

Major del Valle raises his saber; the squad closes ranks around Nachito and the student and moves off.

VI

Bleary-eyed and frazzled, Taracena peered through the barred window. She strove to identify the prisoners, taciturn shadows amid gray crisscrossed bayonets. The sacristan to the nuns poked his head out of the bell tower. Bugles in barracks and forts sounded reveille. The sun made tracks over the sea. Nocturnal itinerants, Indians, entered the city, their llamas laden with fruit from mountain farms. Unruly livestock warmed up in the dawn haze. The port woke to the sound of approaching cowbells; the rifle patrol disappeared with the two prisoners through the Portuguese Mothers Arcade. In the cathouse, Big Mamma shouted at her wards to clean up the mess on the top floor; the pimp with a flower behind his ear was busy changing the soiled sheets. Lupita *la Romántica*, in pink nightgown, prayed before the candlelit altar in the Green Boudoir. The pimp, with a pin between his lips, contemplated piled-up blankets. "I still haven't got over the shock!" he mumbled.

PART FOUR

A Necromantic Amulet

BOOK ONE

The Escape

I

"DAINTY" Domiciano de la Gándara was in a fix. But he'd recalled an Indian who owed him a favor. Slowing down so as not to arouse suspicion, he walked through the Portuguese Mothers Arcade and out onto the Rich Peruvian's Plot.

II

Zacarías San José had a gash on his face so everybody called him Scarface Zac. His shack was in an enormous waterlogged stretch of reeds and dunes that was known as the Rich Peruvian's Plot: turkey buzzards—the *auras* of the Andean plains and the *zopilotes* of the Mexican estuaries—pecked the muddy banks. Horses grazed on the banks of waterways. Meanwhile Zacarías was busy fashioning Chiromayo and Chiromeca tribal funeral deities out of mud. The reeds and dunes seemed to float in the early-morning mist. Pigs wallowed in the mudflats behind the shack. The squatting potter wore a pineapple-leaf sombrero and a long shirt, and he was painting chocolate-brown motifs on pitchers and pots. Taciturn under a cloud of flies, he stared at a dead horse on the far side of the reeds. He felt afraid: a buzzard had got into the roof space, battering it with its black wings, an ill omen. Another ill omen: the paint had run—yellow, meaning bile, and black, meaning jail, or death, had dribbled into each other. And now he remembered: last night his *chinita* put out the fire and found a salamander under the grindstone ... The potter moved his brushes methodically, trapped between thought and action.

III

At the back of the shack, the *chinita* stows her tit in her loose smock and pushes away the child who lies bellowing on the ground. She spanks him. She pulls his ears, lifting him as high as the roof. She stands next to her husband, intent on the brushstrokes he paints on the pot.

"Zac, you're so quiet!"

"What do you want?"

"I haven't got a cent."

"I'll fire the pots today."

"And in the meantime?"

Zacarías smiled sarcastically. "Don't nag! You're meant to fast in Lent."

His brush hangs in the air. Colonel Domiciano de la Gándara stands at the entrance to the hut: finger at his lips.

IV

The barefoot Indian scurries over to the little colonel. Tentative words by the tentacular agave: "Zac, will you help me in a tight spot?"

"Boss, no need to ask!"

"There's a smell of gunpowder in the air. Santos Banderas has turned against me. Can you help?"

"Your wish is my command!"

"How do I get hold of a horse?"

"I'd say there are three ways, chief: buy, borrow, or steal."

"I don't have any money and I don't have any friends. So where do I lasso me one? And there's a posse after me. So tell me, can you take me to Potrero Negrete by canoe?"

"Let's go, chief. My canoe's in the reeds."

"You know you're risking your skin, Zac."

"For what that's worth, boss!"

V

A dog sniffs around the agave's tentacles; the little kid stands next to his mother under the palm fronds. He's whining. He wants some tit. Zacarías waves at his wife to come over. "I'm going with the boss!"

Her voice piped, "Is it a big deal?"

"Looks like it."

"Remember, if you're held up, I'm dead broke."

"What am I supposed to do, baby? You can pawn something."

"Like the blanket off our bed!"

"Pawn your watch."

"They won't give me nothing for a watch with a cracked face!"

Scarface unhooked a nickel pocket watch on a rusty chain. Colonel de la Gándara interjected: "Are you that broke, Zacarías?"

Zac's *chinita* sighed. "He blows it all on cards, chief! His stupid bets cleaned us out!"

"I'm sure it's not worth a boliviano!"

The little colonel dangles the watch on its chain. With a raucous laugh, he flings it into the marshes, by the pigs. "A real friend!"

The *chinita* nodded meekly. She's seen where the watch fell. She'd go and retrieve it later. The little colonel took off his ring. "Here. This might help."

The woman threw herself on the ground. She kissed her savior's hand.

VI

Scarface went to put his pants on along with his pistol and machete belt. His other half follows after. "What a shitty trick it's gonna be if that ring's fake!"

"Yeah, a shitty trick and then some!"

The *chinita* shows him her hand, making the pinchbeck ring flash. "The stones are shiny. The hockshop might give me enough for a little grub."

"If you only try one, they might trick you."

"I'll try a bunch. If it's the real deal, it's got to be worth a hundred pesos—or more."

"Tell them that if it's worth anything, it's worth five hundred."

"I'll take it now, right?"

"And if they pay a lot?"

"Yeah, go on hoping!"

VII

From the doorway, the little colonel surveyed the Rich Peruvian's Plot.

"Hurry."

The Indian was on his way, with his kid in his arms and his *chinita* at his side. She lets out a meek sigh. "When will you be back?"

"Who knows? Light a candle to the Virgin of Guadalupe."

"I'll light two!"

"Good idea!"

He kissed the child goodbye with a sweep of his mustache and stuck him in his mother's arms.

VIII

The little colonel and Zacarías walked along the bank of the big waterway to the Soldiers Well. A feeding trough was stuck in the silt.

Zacarías pushed it into the water, and they continued upstream beneath a canopy of tall reeds and blossoming lianas.

BOOK TWO

The Pinchbeck Ring

I

QUINTÍN PEREDA, PAWNBROKER. Zac's wife stopped in front of the shopwindow: a glittering showcase for earrings, tiepins, and cuff links, topped off with pistols and daggers and draped in lacy silk and lurid linen. She looked long and hard: the baby lay in her shawl that she carried at her hip hammock-like. She wiped the sweat from her brow, put her clothes straight, and tidied her hair, and mumbling a humble litany went through the door. "Hello, boss! I've just dropped in with the prize of the month. It's yours because you're so honest and good! Take a look at this little jewel!"

She laid her brown hand on the counter, with the ring on one finger. Honest whitey Quintín Pereda put his newspaper down on his knees and pushed his spectacles up onto his baldpate. "What's that you've got?"

"Something for you. It's a lovely ring. Just see how it glints, boss."

"You don't expect me to give you a price without you taking it off!"

"Sure. Aren't you the expert?"

"I have to dip the ring in aqua fortis and weigh the stone!"

The *chinita* removed the ring and placed it reverently on whitey's nails. "It all comes down to you, Mr. Peredita."

Crouching by the counter, she kept her eyes glued on the usurer. He stood under the light, examining the ring with a magnifying glass. "I think I recognize this item."

Zac's wife didn't miss a beat. "It's not mine. I'm here to help a white family. They're having a hard time."

The pawnbroker resumed his examination with a tinny laugh. "This little jewel's been here before. You've pinched it."

"Hey, chief, don't try to cheat me!"

The usurer slid his specs down off his pate, laughed another hollow laugh. "My records will show under what name it was put into hock before."

He took a file from the shelf and started leafing through papers. He was a wily old dealer. He knew how to blend sweet talk and innuendo, lies and half-truths. He'd left his homeland as a young kid and combined native guile with the natural suspicion of his kind. His Creole wit was as syrupy as stewed plums. He looked up. Again he pushed his spectacles onto his forehead. "Little Colonel Gandarita pawned this solitaire last August... and redeemed it on October 7. I'll give you five sols."

Zac's wife whistled, holding one hand over her mouth. "How much was it worth? Tell me, boss."

"Don't haggle! I'll give you five sols. It's a special favor. What I should do is inform the gendarmes."

"I'm so unlucky!"

"This item doesn't belong to you. I might give you the five sols and then have to return it to its owner, if he makes a legal claim. I could get into trouble for doing you a favor that you don't even appreciate. I'll give you three sols—and you can get packing."

"Hey, chief, pull the other one!"

The pawnbroker leant sardonically on his counter and declared, "I'll have you arrested."

Zac's wife bounded to her feet, gave him a sharp look, with her kid on her hip and her hands in her hair. "Jesus wept! I told you it's not mine. The colonel sent me."

"I need proof. Take three sols. Don't risk getting stuck in the stocks."

"Chief, give it back."

"You must be joking! Take the three sols, and if I'm wrong, then let the real owner come and clinch the deal. In the meantime, his little item will be on hold here. My name is guarantee enough. Take the cash and scram."

"Hey, Mr. Peredita, this is an insult!"

"And you should be in the stocks!"

"Mr. Peredita, stop the slandering. You've got it all wrong. The colonel's in trouble. He needs money quick. If you don't want to make a deal, give the ring back. Come on, chief, and don't do me wrong. You've always been a nice guy."

"Don't force me to stick by the law. If you don't take your cash and get moving, I'll call the gendarmes."

Zac's *chinita* turned, defiant and desperate. "You're a real white man!"

"Yeah, a proud white man. We don't stand for thieves."

"While you're busy thieving!"

"You're asking for it!"

"You evil bastard!"

"I'll beat your filthy hide!"

"You come from an evil place, to be so high and mighty!"

"Don't insult my fatherland, or I'll really be mad!"

The pawnbroker dips behind the counter and springs back up brandishing a horsewhip.

II

The owlish blind man and the listless wench walked shamefaced into honest whitey's pawnshop. The girl stopped the blind man in front of the red curtain. The man whispered, "Who's he arguing with?"

"Some Indian woman."

"We've come at the wrong time!"

"Well, who can say?"

"We'll come back later."

"To find the same scene. Nothing will have changed."

"So let's wait."

The pawnbroker stepped forward. "Come in. I hope you're bringing what you owe on the piano—three payments."

The blind man muttered, "Solita, inform Mr. Pereda of the situation and of our best intentions."

The girl sighed affectedly. "We'll meet the terms. We're trying to straighten things out."

Whitey responded with a sour smile. "'Trying' isn't enough. There must be action. You're very behindhand. I *like* to take into account my customers' circumstances even if it's not in my interest. That's how I've always done business and some day I will again, but right now this revolution is ruining business. My situation's too bad for me to start relaxing regulations! What can you pay now?"

The blind owl looked back over the girl's shoulder. "Tell him how it is, Solita. Be as eloquent as you can."

The girl muttered sorrowfully, "We haven't been able to get the cash. We wanted to ask if we could have until the end of the month."

"Impossible, sweetheart!"

"Only to the end of the month!"

"I hate to say no. But sweetheart, one must look after oneself, really one must. If you don't pay up, I'll have to repossess the piano—reluctantly. Maybe it'll be a relief—you can forget the payments. You have to look at everything from every side!"

The blind man slunk around the girl. "But won't we lose what we paid?"

The pawnbroker replied in honeyed tones, "Naturally! But I'll cover the moving costs and forgive any wear and tear."

The blind man cowered before him. He muttered, "Give us until the end of the month, Mr. Peredita."

The pawnbroker's tone was more honeyed than ever. "Impossible! I'm ruining myself by being so easygoing! Enough's enough! I've had to harden my soft heart to keep from going bankrupt! If I lose my nerve, you'll drive me into the poorhouse! Until tomorrow, and that's it. Try to sort it out. And don't waste any more of my time."

The girl begged. "Mr. Peredita, to the end of the month!"

"Impossible, my lovely! I'd like nothing more than to say yes!"

"Don't be like your fellow countrymen, Mr. Peredita!"

"Hey, wash your mouth out with bleach when you speak of my country. Don't bitch about Spain, sweetheart, because if it weren't for the land of my fathers you'd still be in parrot feathers."

The blind man doubled over with rage. He told the girl to lead him out. "Spain may be wonderful, but the specimens they send here stink to high heaven."

The pawnbroker cracked his whip on the counter. "Beat it! The fatherland and its offspring cannot be judged by illiterate beggars."

The listless lass tugged on her father's sleeve. "Daddy, don't fly off the handle."

He was tapping the doorway with his metal stick. "That whitey Jew is crucifying us. He's taking your piano away just when you were playing your best!"

III

The other *chinita* with the kid on her hip slips out of the shadows. "Don Quintinito, don't be so mean! Give me back my little ring!"

With one hand she pulls back her shawl; with the other gestures to the listless couple to wait. The pawnbroker cracks his whip on the counter again. "Can't you see you're digging your own grave, you dumb bitch!"

"Give me back my little ring."

"As soon as my assistant returns I'll send him to speak to the real owner. You've got to be patient until everything checks out. My credit should be guarantee enough. In the meanwhile, the little item stays here. Now get going and don't leave me any of your lice."

Zac's *chinita* runs to the door and wails at the listless couple who moan and groan as they disappear down the street. "Just listen to him! Just think how he's robbing me!"

Whitey rummaged in his cashbox and called out, "No need to be so rude. Here's five sols."

"Keep your money and give me my ring."

"Don't get my back up."

"Mr. Peredita, you don't know what you're doing. My Zac'll come after you, and Don Quintinito, his dagger's sharp!"

The pawnbroker stacked five sols on the counter. "There are laws, there are gendarmes, there are prisons, and, in the last resort, there are bullets. I'll pay my dues and rid society of a hoodlum."

"Boss, he won't be an idiot and come in broad daylight."

"Take the money, you peasant. If it turns out I owe you more—once the proper inquiries have been made—I'll give you more. Take the money. If you can pay up when the ticket's due, bring me the money and I'll see if I can give you an extension."

"Boss, stop it! Give me what I'm owed. Colonel Gandarita had to leave town unexpectedly and he left some things to settle. Come on, give what I'm owed!"

"Impossible! I'll give you just over half. Read the rate in the book, nine sols. You're getting more than fifty percent!"

"Mr. Peredita, don't swallow those zeros!"

"Okay, seeing how things stand, I'll give you nine sols. And don't talk back! If you're lying, the owner's going to take me to court!"

Honest whitey whined, and Zac's *chinita* scooped up the nine sols, counting them, passing them from hand to hand before knotting them in the tip of her shawl. Child on hip, she bent to the ground and raced off like a greyhound. "Go to hell, boss!"

"Ungrateful bitch! Like all the rest in this country!"

The pawnbroker hung his whip on a nail, dusted his files, opened the local rag sent from his hometown in Asturias, and began to luxuriate. *The Avilés Echo* catered to honest whitey's love of patriotic gore. News of deaths, marriages, and baptisms reminded him of cider bars with accordion music and nights of anisette and chestnuts. He went into raptures over the court register with its tales of disputed boundaries and crops in rustic haunts. He imagined a rain-sodden countryside: rainbows, wintry storms, sunny intervals, mountain gullies, seas of green.

IV

Melquíades, honest whitey's nephew and assistant, came in at the head of a bunch of young kids. They were ringing the painted clay cowbells that are sold in church entrances on the Day of the Dead. Melquíades was short and squat, with the complacent mug of a rich emigrant sitting on a fortune. These little idiots lined up in front of the counter and tinkled their clay bells. "Forget it, kids, go tinkle for Mamma! Why are you all dressed up? Melquíades, why'd you spoil them, and let them waste their few pennies? A bell for every four would have been enough! These are kids who are used to sharing things. Go to Mamma and get out of your Sunday best."

Melquíades took command of his troops. Directing them up a narrow staircase. "Don Celes Galindo bought the bells for them."

"That's what you call a good friend! Kids, tell Mamma to store these bells away. They're souvenirs—for next year and for years to come. Now don't be naughty!"

At the foot of the stairs Melquíades watched his flock going up, careful not to spoil their new clothes. Tumbling downstairs was for everyday wear. Melquíades elaborated on Don Celes's largesse: "He got them the priciest ones! He took the kids up to the Mothers Arcade and told them to choose. The little rascals wanted the ones that cost most. And Don Celes pulled out his wallet and paid up without blinking. By the way, he urges you to attend the council at the Spanish casino."

"Goddamn him and his bells! I'm still paying off the first installment! They'll put me on a committee. I'll have to leave the shop for hours on end and they'll want a contribution! You always have to pay for these meetings. That's not what the casino is for! That's not what it says in the statutes! It's a place to relax and they've turned it into a machine for extorting money."

"The whole colony is up in arms!"

"And quite right, too! Hey, take the solitaire out of this phony ring. We've got to take it apart."

Melquíades sat down at the counter and looked for tweezers in the drawer.

"The *Criterion* is protesting the foreign legation's demand that bars and liquor stores be closed."

"Of course. Whose interest is that in? Selling liquor's legal and a license costs a pretty penny. Has Don Celestino given his opinion?"

"Don Celes wants all the Spanish businesses to close in protest. That's why there's a meeting of the council at the casino."

"Good luck to him! That's never going to happen. I'll go to the meeting and tell them what I think. They're damaging the interests of the colony as a whole. All over the world trade fulfills an important social function. Unless everybody closes down, somebody is just losing business. If the minister for Spain does go along with shutting down the bars, he's going to find he's extremely unpopular here in the colony. How does Don Celestino see it?"

"He didn't mention the minister's position."

"The council of worthies needs to clamp down on that oddball. Prod him in the right direction, and if he doesn't take the hint, send a telegram demanding his removal. Now that's something I'd push for."

"Who wouldn't?"

"So get on with it, you rascal."

"So tell me what to do and I'll do it."

"Why do you always argue, Melquíades? Always! One telegram would set everything straight. A sodomite, the talk of the town, with his little boy toy behind bars at this very moment!"

"No, they've let him out. The gendarmes have locked up Baby Roach. There's a revolution brewing!"

"The people behind this rumpus don't have their papers in order at the consulate. Anyway Roach and her vile trade are a blot on the good name of the fatherland."

"Baby's really messed up this time. She's implicated in Colonel Gandarita's escape."

"So little Colonel Gandarita escaped. Put that ring down right away! It's hot. Escaped from Santa Mónica?"

"He escaped when they went to arrest him this morning in Baby Roach's cathouse!"

"On the run! Zac's bitch sure hoodwinked me! Drop those tweezers! On the run! Colonel Gandarita in a pickle outside the law! Goddamn that *chinita* and her story! Melquíades, that solitaire's Colonel Gandarita's! That drunken idiot's lassoed me tight! Got nine sols out of me!"

Melquíades gave a sullen smile. "Well, it's worth five hundred!"

Honest whitey turned vinegary. "Fuck that. I'm going to have to take a loss if I want to stay out of trouble. I'm off to police headquarters to tell what happened. They'll probably want me to hand over the ring."

Honest whitey shook his head as he ruminated on the fickleness of the world and fortune.

V

Honest whitey stoops down behind the counter and changes out of his slippers into new boots. Then he locks the drawers and unhooks his screw-pine-leaf sombrero from a nail. "I'm going now."

Melquíades was against it. "Keep your mouth shut and don't let on."

"We'll have the gendarmes here any minute! You're only good for stuff and nonsense, Melquíades! Your advice is worth nothing in this kind of jam! The gendarmes will know what's up and I wouldn't be surprised if they hadn't got their hands on that scheming bitch already. I'll be implicated if I don't abide by Generalito Banderas's decrees and report what's happened. Do you want to risk breaking the law? I trusted that woman, and now it's cost me nine sols. That's where it gets you if you don't keep your conscience locked in the cellar. I was going to give that cheating slut three sols, but she screwed me out of nine. Nephew, if you want to prosper in this line of business, you've got to watch out or you'll never make a cent. In Spain they think all you've got to do is scratch the surface to make a mint over here! If I don't want problems, I'm going to have to hand over the ring and kiss nine sols goodbye."

"When you go to tell the gendarmes, why not hand them a much less valuable item?" Melquíades asked, with the astute smirk of an Asturian farmhand.

Honest whitey gaped at his nephew. A sudden, consoling light lit up the old fellow's soul. "'A much less valuable item!'"

BOOK THREE
The Little Colonel

I

ZACARÍAS steered the canoe to Lake Ticomaipú under a canopy of tall bulrushes. A joyous racket of brass, rockets, and baseball enlivened the morning. The Indians were celebrating All Saints' Day. Bells pealed. Zacarías stowed the oars, slung his boathook into the silt, ran the skiff aground, and tied it to the spiny cactus that fenced in a yard for hens, turkeys, and pigs. The Indian muttered, "We're in Kid Filomeno territory."

"That's good news. Put your head out."

"The boss must be living it up in town."

"See if he's about."

"What if he's scared of getting involved?"

"Filomeno's a good friend."

"But what if he's scared and orders my arrest?"

"That's not going to happen."

"You gotta to be ready for the worst, chief. Anyway I'm here to serve you. I'll keep quiet and do what you say no matter how they tighten the screws."

The colonel chuckled. "If you've got any other bright ideas, just let me know. You're no idiot."

The Indian was peering over the fence. "If Kid Filomeno isn't here, I reckon we should rustle his horses and scram."

"Where to?"

"The rebel camp."

"I need cash for the ride."

The colonel jumped out of the boat and scrambled up the mud bank. He stood by the Indian and peered over the fence. The church belfry and its tricolor flag stuck out above the palms and cedars. Irrigation channels and fences divided the land into little plots that spread out over the freshly ploughed reddish soil and the various shades of green. Herds of livestock grazed in the distance. Horses chomped on the banks of the waterways. They could hear the splashing oars of an approaching canoe. A gray-whiskered Indian, in a big palm-frond sombrero and a canvas shirt, was rowing: Kid Filomeno sat in the poop. The canoe docked by a wooden gate. The colonel stepped forward to greet the farmer. "Hello, I'm here in time for breakfast. I see you're an early riser!"

The farmer was suspicious. "I spent the night in town. I went to hear what Don Roque Cepeda had to say."

They hugged each other tight, lifting each other off the ground in turn. Old friends.

II

The colonel and Filomeno walked side by side down a path through a grove of lemon and orange trees and out in front of a large farmhouse: it had a portico with whitewashed arches and a saint from Almagro whose halo lit up the floor tiles. A large number of birdcages and the owner's hammock hung from the portico beams. Blue creepers covered the walls. The two men slumped down on adjacent *jinocales* under the arched doorway in front of a little curtain with a Japanese lily pattern. The boss ordered his gray-bearded servant to bring out the breakfast meats and told the maid, a black Mandinga, to brew some maté. Old China returned with a plate of hung mutton. He explained in Cutumay that the farmer's wife and children weren't there because they'd gone to church. The boss simply waved his hand and offered his guest some jerky. The colonel speared a slice of meat with a knife he'd taken from his belt, dropped it on his plate, and raised his flagon of maize beer. He downed three gulps for Dutch courage and declared, "I'm in a hell of a spot!"

"Tell me."

"I've set out to do that bastard Banderas in. I've dealt myself a shit hand, as the Holy Fathers say. My friend, I'm poorer than the poorest down-and-out, and there's a tyrant on my trail. I'm going to rebel territory to fight for my country's freedom, Filomeno, and I've come to seek your help, since you're not exactly Santos Banderas's buddy. Will you help?"

The farmer's dark eyes stared at little Colonel de la Gándara. "You've got what you deserved! For fifteen years we've endured the oppression you're now condemning. What were you doing all that time? You never remembered our country when you were in Banderas's good graces. And I bet you don't now, I bet you're just hoping you'll prize some little secret out of me. Banderas has turned every one of you into a spy."

The little colonel jumped up. "Go ahead, Filomeno, stick the knife in, but don't sink me in the mud! Even the dregs have their saintly moments. And that's how it is with me now. I'm ready to spill my last drop of blood to save our country."

"I don't know what your fool idea is, Domiciano. I leave that to your conscience. You can't do me much harm, ready as I am to set my farm on fire and take up arms with my peons. That's not news to you. I was at last night's rally and with my own eyes I saw them lead off Don Roque Cepeda in handcuffs, between two horses. I heard the righteous outrage of the people and the insults of the gendarmes!"

The little colonel's eyes sparkled: his ruddy cheeks puffed out into a broad grin—like a bloated idol with one hell of a beer gut. "Filomeno, there's no legal protection for our citizens. It's a sick joke. Don Roque Cepeda isn't going to see the sun rise many more times once he's locked up in Santa Mónica. The poor are on his side, but he hasn't kowtowed to the military, and he'll never be elected president with only Indian votes. What he needs is a revolution! I've been betrayed, and I'll tell it to them straight before they execute me. Together we can knock the stuffing out of Generalito Banderas! Filomeno, my friend, you're a greenhorn when it comes to fighting. Listen to an expert! I'll appoint you as my aide-de-camp. Filomeno, just have your maid sew on a captain's stripe."

Filomeno Cuevas smiled: he was dark-eyed and aquiline, with wolfish teeth and a jet-black mustache and eyebrows: a steely, noble, handsome mien. "Domiciano, it would be a fucking shame if my peons refused to recognize you as their chief and killed you just like Banderas ordered."

The colonel gulped. He was upset. "Filomeno, you're not being a good citizen. You're pulling my leg."

The other laughed. "You've got talent, Domiciano, I can see that. I'll make you my company bugler—at least, if you know your scales."

"Don't twist the knife, friend! Given my situation, your jokes are in terrible taste. I'm not going to take a lower rank than you. Let's say goodbye, Filomeno. I hope you won't refuse me a horse and a guide. I could also use some cash."

Filomeno Cuevas looked friendly enough, but his lips curled in a sardonic smile as he put his hand on the colonel's shoulder. "Keep calm. You haven't had a chance to speak to my peons yet. I'll make you leader if they want you. One way or another, let's join forces now. We can sort things out after we've taken action."

Little Colonel de la Gándara raised himself to his full height, prancing and bantering with his farmer buddy. "Hey, you're not doing me any favors by squabbling over a bunch of Indians. You lead them to the slaughter: You're their boss. You pay them. Stop playing the fool and get me that horse. If they find me here, we'll both be bound for Santa Mónica. There are bloodhounds on my heels!"

"If they show their snouts, we'll be warned soon enough. I know what's at stake. They're not going to catch me napping like a bug in a rug."

The colonel nodded, suitably impressed. "That means there's time for another beer. If you've posted sentinels you're thinking ahead—just like a soldier. Congratulations, Filomeno!"

With the neck of the canteen between his lips he sprawled on his *jinocal*, his belly as big as a Tibetan god's.

III

The chatter of little voices brought cheer to the empty house and gloomy deserted rooms. Children were playing and jumping gleefully. In a cloud of priestly incense, the lady of the ranch walked in and unpinned her cape. The kids scattered around her. Colonel de la Gándara snored on the *jinocal*, legs sprawled before him, his beer gut rising and falling as regularly as the earth goes around. The lady of the ranch exchanged glances with her husband. "Who's our apostle?"

"He turned up looking for a safe haven. He says he's fallen out of favor. His name's on the blacklist."

"What happened to you last night? I waited up because I was so worried!"

The rancher fell silent and looked somber. His dark steely eyes softened in the warm light. "Laurita, you and the kids are keeping me from doing my duty as a citizen! The most wretched peasant in the rebel camp is more patriotic than Filomeno Cuevas. I've decided to break the fetters of family. I'm not going to stand on the sidelines any longer. Listen to me, Laurita. I feel like a rank coward compared to the lowest soldier in the revolutionary army. Why weep for me? Laurita, I'm doing business as usual while others risk their lives and wealth in defense of freedom. I saw Don Roque led away between bayonets last night. If I don't get my hands dirty and pick up a rifle, it's because I don't have any guts or I don't have any shame. No, Laurita, I've made up my mind. No tears!"

Once again the rancher fell silent, though his eyes had their eagle glint again. His wife leaned back against a column and covered her eyes with her shawl. Adrift in an alcoholic haze, the colonel opened his eyes and yawned, jolted from deep sleep into delirious reality. He saw the lady of the house. Garlanded with the laurels of Bacchus and Mars, he rose to greet her heart to heart.

IV

Old China signaled to his boss from over the gate. Two bridled horses pricked up their ears. The rancher and his overseer spoke briefly, mounted their steeds, and cantered off.

BOOK FOUR

Honest Whitey

I

HONEST whitey didn't waste any time. He headed straight to police headquarters. Following his nephew's shrewd advice, he gave his statement and handed over in evidence a lousy solitaire so low in carats that even by the wildest overestimation it wasn't worth ten sols. Colonel López de Salamanca praised his civic spirit. "Don Quintín, I can't thank you enough for your forthright contribution to this investigation. Rushing to our office in order to supply us with such invaluable information—I congratulate you on such praiseworthy behavior. But could I beg you to elaborate on a few of the details? Are you personally acquainted with the village woman who brought the ring? Do you have any idea where she lives? That would be a great help in capturing the aforesaid. Most likely the fugitive met the said female when he discovered that a warrant had been issued for his arrest. Do you believe he sought her out with a specific purpose in mind?"

"Possibly."

"They didn't meet by chance?"

"Who knows?"

"Do you know the whereabouts of this lowlife's abode?"

"No clue."

II

Honest whitey was covering his back so as not to blow it and get hurt. He was afraid he might get in a tangle, tipping them off to the trick he'd pulled. The chief of police stared at him, smiling suspiciously and superciliously, the infallible skewering by a uniformed telepath. The pawnbroker began to panic and cursed Melquíades under his breath. "We enter every receipt. I'll take a look. I can't guarantee my assistant has got around to it yet. He's a careless young fellow who's only just come from the mother country."

The chief of police stuck out his chest and leaned over his desk. "What a shame if you got hit with a big fine because of some careless fool."

The pawnbroker concealed his annoyance. "Dear Colonel, if he *has* been negligent, there are ways and means for your men to get the goods. That peasant lives with a no-good who's visited my establishment more than once. I'm sure he's on your books. Hardly a law-abiding citizen. One of those bandits who was amnestied years ago—when a deal was done with the ringleaders and they were given an army stripe. Nowadays he sets up as a potter."

"Do you happen to know this individual's name?"

"I expect it will come to me."

"Any distinguishing feature?"

"A scar over his face."

"Scarface Zac?"

"I'd hate to be wrong, but yes, that could be him."

"You show great insight, Mr. Peredita. I must reiterate my thanks. We're on the right path now. You may go."

Honest whitey inquired: "And the little ring?"

"We must attach it to the statement."

"So I lose nine sols?"

"Your tough luck! But you can put in an appeal to the Justice Department. There'll be some red tape but I'm sure you'll get compensation in the end. Start the appeal now. We'll be in touch, Mr. Peredita!"

The chief of police rang his bell. A sweaty, shabby clerk walked in: creased starched collar, tie at half-mast, pen behind ear, an ink-stained drill guayabera with black half sleeves. The colonel scribbled on a docket, stamped it, and handed it to the clerk. "Proceed to the immediate arrest of this couple. Choose men who are ready to shoot and tell them to be on high alert: Scarface Zac's a genuine tough guy. If someone who knows him is available, give him the job. And pull Zac's file. We'll be in touch, Mr. Peredita. You've been most helpful!"

He dispatched him with a round of flattering flimflam. Honest whitey withdrew, crestfallen, directing one last, lingering glance, like a whimpering pooch, at the table where the ring was irrevocably marooned under a sea of forms. After instructing the clerk, the chief of police peered out the barred window overlooking the courtyard. A squad of gendarmes lined up and rushed off. The corporal, a handlebar-mustachioed mestizo, was a veteran of the old campaign against the brigands led by Colonel Irineo Castañon, Peg Leg.

III

The corporal stationed his men in pairs around the shack on the Rich Peruvian's Plot. He peered around the door, pistol cocked. "Zac, give yourself up!"

The *chinita*'s tremulous voice came from inside: "That no-good bum's gone and left me! You won't find him here! The beast's looking for fresh pastures!"

Her shadow cowered behind a grindstone, as she whined and whimpered and made herself scarce. The gendarmes converged on the door, aiming their pistols inside. The corporal rasped, "Outside now!"

"Why do you want me?"

"To put a flower in your hair."

The corporal cracked jokes to keep up his men's spirits. The barefoot mother, child on hip, emerged meekly from the darkness, her hair trailing over her shoulders. "You can search every nook and cranny. That bum's gone and left his kids with nothing but his sandals."

"Listen, baby, we know what's doing. Cut the crap. You pawned a ring that belonged to Colonel de la Gándara."

"It was pure chance that ended up with me! I found it."

"You are summoned to appear before my immediate superior, Colonel López de Salamanca. Put the child down and get a move on."

"Can't I take my child with me?"

"Police headquarters isn't a home for waifs and strays."

"What am I supposed to do with my kid?"

"We'll arrange admission to a charitable institution."

The kid crawled out between the gendarme's legs and toddled off toward the marsh. His mother cried anxiously, "You bad boy, come back!"

Pointing his gun, the corporal entered the dark hovel. "Watch out! Who wants to volunteer to search the place? Be on the lookout. The bum could be hiding in there waiting to take a potshot. Surrender, Scarface! Don't fuck around. You'll only make things worse for yourself."

He went into the shack, surrounded by gendarmes, his gun pointed ahead into the darkness.

IV

After completing their search, the corporal and his men came out to handcuff the whimpering *chinita*. She sat slumped against the doorway moaning, with her skirts over her head. The corporal yanked her to her feet. Her child was lying in the swamp slime, crying, surrounded by grunting hogs. The gendarmes were pushing and shoving the mother. She twisted around and screamed at the boy, "Come here! Don't be afraid! Come here! Quick!"

The child ran then stopped. He called out to his mother. A gendarme turned, scaring the boy, who froze in place. He was crying and hitting himself in the face. His mother shouted hoarsely, "Come here! Come, come!"

But the child wouldn't budge. He stood on the bank of the waterway and sobbed, watching the distance grow between him and his mother.

BOOK FIVE
The Rancher

I

FILOMENO Cuevas and Old China tied their horses up in front of a shack and pushed in under a flap of cloth. Other ranchers began to arrive in clusters, resplendent in their riding tackle and tall sombreros. They were the owners of neighboring farms, covert supporters of the revolutionary cause. Filomeno Cuevas had given the green light to meet. These associates had already smuggled him arms—a supply lay buried in Potrero Negrete—and there was urgent need to distribute the rifles and cartridge belts among his Indians. Gangers and overseers, Indian scouts and lariat throwers gradually rode in from their respective farms. Filomeno joked and humored everyone as he sized up the rally. He was, he said, in favor of riding into the bush right away. Secretly, he had already made the decision to hand out the rifles, which were hidden in the jungle, to the peons, but for now was careful to keep his plans to himself. The Creole ranchers argued heatedly and voiced their fears. They recognized their colleague's determination and they would help him with horses, peons, and money, but they wanted to do it as stealthily as possible in case Tyrant Banderas should prevail. Dositeo Velasco, one of the wealthiest landowners, seemed an unlikely candidate for this kind of risky business, but he stoked up on coffee and maize beer and started cursing Tyrant. "Fuck you Banderitas, we'll cover the republic with your flayed hide!"

Coffee, grog, and meat pasties had excited the revolutionary choristers, and they all bellowed similar sentiments, did a boisterous business in rich repartee, then exchanged mellifluous apologies for going too far. They were all good friends and gleefully sang dirty limericks to prove it.

"Hey buddy!"

"Hey pal!"

"See ya!"

"See ya!"

They bawled out final farewells, bestrode their saddles, turned their horses, and galloped pell-mell over the vast horizon of the plains.

II

The morning sun poured down on freshly ploughed red earth, where new crops were sprouting, and poured down on the twisted oaks and wild thickets in whose shade steaming bulls lay stretched out. Lake Ticomaipú, surrounded by Indian huts, mirrored the flaming sheaves. The boss gallops along the bank of a creek on a lively dapple gray, behind him his overseer drives his nag furiously on. Clanging bells and shooting rockets brighten the torrid morning. Canoes full of Indians festooned with bunting, branches, and garlands of flowers trail up and down the waterways. Other light boats almost turn over from all the merrymaking. In the lead boat, under a canopy, a troupe of cimarrons—with cardboard masks, spears, and bucklers—dance jubilantly. A drum and a cornet play as they posture and pirouette. The homestead looms in the distance. The green foliage of shady orange groves shimmers. Tiles, terraces, and roofs sparkle. Eager to reach the farm, the horse breaks into a fresh gallop. The overseer slides the gate open, stands in his stirrups, and looks around: under an arch the colonel, in his hammock, strums a guitar and encourages some kids to dance; two coppery maids, in low-necked nightshirts, laugh and joke behind the bars of the kitchen window and the pots of geraniums from El Sardinero. Filomeno Cuevas prances on his dapple gray and flicks its haunch with his whip. The horse bounds through the gate. "Hit it, friend! You're better than that gaucho Santos Vega any day!"

"Speak for yourself! . . . So what happened? Are you going to let them catch me? Made up your mind?"

The boss leapt off his steed, entered the porch, clattering his silver spurs, his many-colored poncho slung across his shoulder: the embroidered brim of his sombrero threw his aquiline features and goatee in shadow. "'Dainty' Domiciano, I'll supply you with fifty bolivars, a guide, and a horse so you can get going. When you were buzzing on before, I said we'd ride together. But I've had a change of heart. As to the fifty bolivars, you'll get those as soon as you're safe behind revolutionary lines. You will travel unarmed and your guide is under orders to plug you if you do anything suspicious. My friend, I'd advise you to say nothing, because the order is a secret."

The little colonel sat up calmly. He silenced his sorrowing guitar. "Don't try to put one over on me, Filomeno! You know my honor won't allow me to accept such humiliating terms. I didn't expect such treatment from you! You've gone from being my friend to being my jailer!"

With graceful forbearance, Filomeno Cuevas threw his hat and poncho on a *jinocal*. He pulled a fine silk handkerchief out of his pocket and wiped the sweat off his weather-beaten features and gleaming white forehead framed by dark locks of hair. "Don't fuck up! Domiciano! Take what you can get. Don't try to dictate terms."

The little colonel opened his arms. "Filomeno, your heart knows no generosity!"

He was hopelessly hammered, and his boastful blather was full of tropical heat. The boss headed over to his hammock cracking jokes all the time, stretched out, grabbed the guitar, and started tuning. "I'll save your life, Domiciano! But I'm playing it safe until I know it's in danger for real: and if you're a spy, believe me, you're going to die. Old China will conduct you safely behind rebel lines, and they can decide what to do with you. As a matter of fact—I've got an urgent message to send to them. You and Old China are going to take it for me. Yeah. I meant to make you my bugle boy but somehow the dice didn't fall that way."

The little colonel gave himself martial airs. "Filomeno, I am your prisoner, I know. I won't lower myself by arguing about terms. My life is in your hands; take it if you wish. You'll be giving these little ones a fine lesson in hospitality. Children, don't be afraid. Come here, come learn how to welcome a friend who, with nothing to his name and a murderous tyrant on his trail, seeks shelter under your roof."

And the little ones gathered around, their innocent eyes wide with fear and suspense. Suddenly a girl standing right in the middle of the group flounced her dressy skirt and burst into sobs. The two gangling kids beside her looked on astonished. She had been overwhelmed by the colonel's showpiece. Her grandmother rushed out, a swarthy old lady with Italian blood and a white chignon, coal-black eyes, and a beak as big as Dante's. "Cosa c'é, amore?"

But the little colonel had already seized the girl, kissing her and rubbing his beard all over her face. He drew up his great round girth and held the weeping wonder in his arms, so that his raised gluttonous face was foreshortened into a caricature of Saturn. The girl starts struggling and crying. She wants to escape, and her grandmother standing next to the Japanese curtain with her shawl hanging crooked is on the verge of collapse. Drunkenly the little colonel goads her: "Don't get your knickers in a twist, old girl. It'll give you a heart attack!"

"Don't upset *la bambina*!"

"Filomeno, explain the joke to your mother-in-law. Explain what you have been taught by this little angel. Don't try to get out of it; tell her! Be your usual bold self!"

III

The five kids sway in sweet harmony. The little colonel sprawls in their midst, while his grotesque face wrinkles up into a frown. He sobs, chest pumping like a balloon. "Tender shoots, you are teaching your parents manners! Children, do not forget this lesson when you grow up and have to make difficult decisions of your own. Filomeno, these tender buds, they will hound you with remorse because of how you have treated me, Domiciano de la Gándara, a dear friend—and not a trace of pity in your heart! He expected a brother's embrace. He was given less welcome than a prisoner of war. Refused arms. Disrespected. Filomeno, you treat me like a bastard, not a brother!"

The boss continued to tune his guitar. He nodded at his mother-in-law to get the kids out of there and the Italian crone herded her flock inside. Filomeno Cuevas clasped his hands behind his back, his eyes beady and sharp. There was a smug smile on his purple lips. "Domiciano, you're not in parliament giving a speech. No doubt you'd bring the roof down if you were. But I'm unfortunately not clever enough to appreciate your oratory. I've made you my final offer."

A long-haired Indian, wrapped in a blanket, his face hidden in shadow by his straw sombrero, came up to his boss and whispered in his ear. Filomeno turned to the little colonel. "We're done for. Federal troops are surrounding the ranch."

The little colonel spat. Looking over his shoulder, he said, "Go on, turn me in, get in Banderas's good books. Filomeno, you don't have any honor left to lose!"

"No more shit! You know perfectly well I stand up for my friends. I had to be careful given your past alliance with Tyrant. We're in a tight spot now, though, and if I don't save you, I'll lose my own head."

"Give me money and a horse."

"Listen, you're not taking off."

"Let me get into the open country on a good horse."

"You're staying here until nightfall."

"Just give me a horse!"

"I'm not going to because I'm doing my best to save you. You're going to stay in a pigsty where the devil himself won't ever find you."

He dragged the colonel off through the shadowy porch.

IV

Another Indian scuttled in, crossing himself. He tiptoed barefoot over to the boss. "The press-gang's out and about. They almost roped me in. They're beating the drum by the church."

The rancher smiled and slapped his friend Domiciano on the shoulder. "I'm playing it safe, yup. Time to put you in that sty."

BOOK SIX

The Lasso

I

SCARFACE Zac tied the skiff to a clump of bulrushes and stood up. He looked at the shack. A flat expanse of inlets and sand dunes, crisscrossed by creeks and flapping waterfowl, spread out before him. In between, there were canebrakes and fields dotted with glistening horses and bulls. The echoes of country life rose up and vanished into the vast sonorous dome of the heavens. A chorus of pigs grunted under the turquoise sky. A dog yelped, pitifully. Startled, Zac whistled at it to come. The dog ran over: fretful, eager to be picked up, upset by something. Zac held it to his chest where it whimpered miserably. Now it tugs at his shirt, drags him out of the skiff. Pulling out his pistol, Scarface walks forward, serious, his breath bated. The shack stands open, silent, and Zac walks past it and goes on down into the swamp; the dog is leading him, its ears pricked, its snout jutting forward, a mass of pathetic shivering panting fur: Zac follows close behind. Pigs grunt in the mud. Chickens cower under the agave's tentacles. The dog barks and buzzards sweep into the sky, their black wings flapping above the swamp slime. And Zac stands there, horrified, grim-faced, lifting up a bloody mess. It is all that is left of his child! Face and hands devoured by pigs; heart pecked out by buzzards. The Indian goes back to the hut. He puts the remains in a bag and sets it down at his feet. He thinks. He's standing completely still. Flies settle on his body. Lizards sunbathe at his side.

II

Zac stood up, full of dark foreboding. He went to the grindstone, turned it over, and saw a dull glimmer of metal. The receipt from the pawnbroker, folded four times, lay underneath. The grimace on his Indian mask remained unchanged as he counted the nine coins, dropped the money in his pouch, and read the note: "Quintín Pereda. Loans. Sales and Purchases." Zac returned to the entrance to the shack, slung the bag over his shoulder and set out for the city. With drooping tail and head, the dog nuzzled alongside. Zac passed down a street of flat-roofed squat houses garlanded in colored bunting, into the noise and lights of the fair. At a stall he bet all nine coins on lansquenet; he doubled his stake and kept winning. An absurd thought hit him—another grisly omen—that bag of bones draped over his shoulder was bringing him luck! He moved on, dog in tow, turned into a bar, and sat there drinking firewater, the bag between his feet. The girl and blind man were eating at a nearby table. Bums and beggar women, Indians from the outback, old dears in search of a tlaco's worth of cumin for their cobs. Zac ordered a ptarmigan stew and left scraps on his plate for his dog. He continued to drink, the brim of his sombrero down low over his face. The idea that those remnants were protection against danger was chilling: he knew they'd be out after him, but he wasn't frightened: a cruel certainty had frozen his heart. He slung the bag of bones over his shoulder and kicked his dog. "Porfirio, let's go pay whitey a visit!"

III

Zac stopped and sat down again. He eavesdropped on the owlish couple's whispers.

"Won't Mr. Peredita give us longer?"

"Don't get your hopes up, dear!"

"If he hadn't been fighting with that Indian woman, he'd have been more sympathetic."

With his straw hat over his face and his bag of bones on his knees, Zac listened carefully. The blind man had taken out a folder full of scraps of paper. He was checking them over—as if those sad fingernails of his could see. "Read me the terms again. There has to be something in our favor."

He handed the girl a sheet that was covered with stipulations and stamps. "We sure do like living in cloud cuckoo land, don't we, Poppa! Whitey has stitched us up."

"Read me the terms."

"I know it by heart. We're done for, Father dear, if we can't get up-to-date with our payments!"

"What do we owe?"

"Seven pesos."

"These are wretched times! In other years picking up seven pesos at the fiestas would have been a piece of cake! The takings from a night like last night would have been three times that!"

"When have things been any different?"

"You're only a child."

"I'll be old soon enough."

"Maybe we should go back and appeal to Mr. Peredita again. We could explain that before long you'll be singing on stage! Isn't that a great idea? Let's go now!"

"Now!"

"You say that so hopelessly!"

"Hopeless is how I feel."

"My love, you're not much consolation! Mr. Peredita may have a heart!"

"He's a whitey!"

"There are good whiteys, too."

"He'll tighten the noose, mercilessly. He's cheap!"

"Well he's been more considerate on other occasions... But he was really furious with that *chinita*, and since they took her away, well, he must have been in the right."

"Somebody else paying for Domiciano's sins!"

IV

Zac edged closer to the listless pair. The blind man realized the girl wasn't going to read the papers and put them back in a black oilskin folder. The owl's face was wan and resigned. The girl pushed her plate over to Zac's dog. Bright-Eyes insisted: "Domiciano screwed us! If it weren't for him, Taracena would be sitting pretty. She could have lent us something or at least been a guarantor."

"Unless he turned her down."

"Please, darling, just an ounce of hope! I'm going to go order a bottle of beer. Don't say no! We'll take it home and I'll finish that waltz I'm going to dedicate to Generalito Banderas."

"Daddy, you just want to get sloshed!"

"Darling, I just need some consolation."

Zac picked up his bottle and filled the glasses of the blind man and the girl. "Get pissed as newts. It's the only way to endure this lousy life. What happened to the *chinita*? Did someone rat her out?"

"Her bad luck!"

"And was it that fucking whitey?"

"Yeah. He didn't want to be implicated himself."

"So that's how it was. Leave Peredita to me."

He slung the bag over his shoulder and left, dog in tow, the brim of his sombrero pulled low over his face.

V

Scarface threaded his way through the circle of ox drivers and cow-punchers drinking on horseback outside the bar. His face was set in a green mask of prickly gloom and grief pounded his temples as he entered the horse fair. Everybody was wrangling and haggling. Stalls sold tackle, knives, and brightly colored ponchos under branches of cedar and palm. Zac crossed over to a broad, dusty sidewalk crowded with food carts. Cowboys from Veracruz showed off their mounts in spirited races. They placed bets and bragged loudly about their horses, hoping they'd be able to pull a fast one. Zac stood under a cedar tree, his feet covered in dust, and took a good look at a roan that a cowpoke was putting through its paces. He felt his winnings under his belt. "You selling that bronco?"

"Yep, he's for sale."

"What do you want?"

"Nothing much."

"Cut the crap, how about fifty bolivianos?"

"Per horseshoe."

Zac kept to his tune. "Fifty bolivianos! You want to sell or what?"

"I'm not giving him away!"

"And I'm not going up."

Zac's expression and tone of voice never changed; he repeated his offer in a monotone like dripping water. The cowpoke put the horse through a series of neat jumps. "Look what he does with barely a nudge—look at his head. Not a trace of strain!"

Zac sang the same tune. "What I'm looking at are fifty bolivianos. Sixty with the tackle."

The cowboy bent down over the saddle horn and patted the horse on the neck soothingly. He half conceded: "Seventy and the drinks are on me."

"Sixty with the saddle, and you can leave me the rope and spurs."

The countryman answered excitedly, keen to strike a deal: "Sixty-five! This horse is a real jewel, pal!"

Zac put his bag down, undid his belt, and, sitting in the shadow of the cedar, counted the money out on a corner of his poncho. Clouds of flies blackened his sticky, bloodstained bag. His bleary-eyed dog sniffed around the horse. The cowpoke dismounted. Zac knotted the money in the corner of his poncho, and got up to check the bronco's hocks and mouth. He jumped into the saddle and rode him up and down, pulling sharply on the reins and bridle, as if he were lassoing a bull. Shading his eyes, the cowpoke stood aside and watched. Zac reined the horse in and rode back. "He'll do fine."

"A jewel!"

Zac undid the corner of his poncho and counted the coins into the cowpoke's palm. "Be seeing you!"

"Buddy, you want to have a quick one to seal the deal?"

"No time, pal. I'm in a rush."

"Too bad."

"Got to get back to my place. Let's have a drink some other time. Be seeing you!"

"Yes, see you! And take care of my roan."

Luminous harmonies of shimmering color vibrated across the fairground. Flocks of llamas, herds of cows, and bands of horsemen undulated along twilight paths of red earth as the sun set over sombreros stitched with silver. Zac spurred his mount out of the madding crowd and headed down the Portuguese Mothers Arcade.

VI

Scarface Zac pulled the brim of his sombrero down low over his face. An awful decision darkened his soul; a single thought drilled at his temples, insistent like his grief. In his mind it was hardening into a simple symmetrical phrase: "Mr. Peredita, you're done for! You're done for, Mr. Peredita!"

He crossed himself whenever he rode past a church. Freak shows were lighting oil lamps. His horse quivered nervously as they rode past a wild-animal menagerie: in a rush of flesh and blood, a tiger reared and roared, pressing its furious head against the iron bars of its cage, eyes on fire, tail thrashing. Zac spurred his horse forward. Covered up by his poncho, his dreadful burden rested against the saddle horn. Zac was mesmerized by the hammer beat of that single throbbing sickening thought. All the time the same words droned in his head: "Mr. Peredita, you're done for! You're done for, Mr. Peredita!"

The streets flashed by, vibrating with the strident cries of hustlers and the sound of guitars, with lantern light and streamers. A barrage of shouts, a mad stampede, a steaming crowd standing hypnotized by catchy tunes. Scarface ignored all the squabbling and speechifying. Coppery beggars straggled along under the lurid illuminations or lingered outside the bars and liquor stores. Their faces fused into a single monstrous face set off by the tawdry glitter of trash trinkets. Dancing, music, bunting fluttering absurdly in the air: an ominous, insane, pent-up chimera. Sunk in rancorous, taciturn despondency, Zac felt a single stubborn thought, a simple symmetrical phrase, whir around his head: "Mr. Peredita, you're done for! You're done for, Mr. Peredita!"

VII

QUINTÍN PEREDA, PAWNBROKER lit up the street from behind the panes of the shopwindow, though cracked glass made the sign illegible. The red and yellow of a percaline Spanish flag decorated the door. The counter inside was lit up by a lamp with a green-tasseled shade. The pawnbroker was stroking his cat, an aging ginger Maltese with a preposterous likeness to its owner. Cat and pawnbroker looked at the door and shuddered simultaneously. The cat on whitey's knees arched its back then settled down, its symmetrical velvet paws on two new mends. Mr. Peredita was in shirtsleeves, a pen behind his ear, wearing a greasy cap that his little girl had embroidered for him years ago at school. "Good evening, boss!"

Scarface Zac—poncho and sombrero, horsehide boots and spurs—bent down low and rode his horse halfway over the threshold. Honest whitey gave him a poisonous glance. "What can I do for you?"

"Just a word in your ear."

"Tie your hoss up outside."

"It's not broken in, boss."

Mr. Peredita walked out from behind the counter. "What business brings you here?"

"Just wanted to meet you, boss! You're famous where I come from. Just wanted to get to know you! That's the only reason I came to the fair, Mr. Peredita."

"You've had a skinful, you tramp. Don't bother honest citizens. Clear off before I call the night watchman."

"Take it easy, Mr. Peredita. I want to redeem a little jewel."

"Have you got the receipt?"

"Just take a look at this!"

Scarface rode his horse all the way in and dropped the dripping, bloodstained bag on the counter with a thud. Whitey was afraid. "You're plastered! You get blind drunk and then you want to make trouble. Clear off and take your little bag with you."

Scarface's head almost touched the roof beams. A shadow fell over his face and chest. His hands and the saddle horn stood out in the light from the counter. "But Mr. Peredita, didn't you say you wanted to see the receipt?"

"Stop messing with me!"

"Please open the bag!"

"Clear off and stop this nonsense."

Grimly Scarface insisted, his voice faint as he seethed inside. "Boss, won't you please take a look and see for yourself."

"I couldn't care less. Goat or pig, the only man fit to eat that is you."

Whitey shrunk from Scarface's descending shadow.

"Try opening the bag with your teeth, Mr. Peredita!"

"Look, asshole, don't play the pesty gaucho with me. If you want to do business, come back when you're sober."

"Boss, we can settle up in a jiffy. Do you remember that Indian girl who pawned a nickel ring for nine bolivianos?"

Honest whitey looked stunned, then cunning. "No, I don't. I'd have to check the books. Nine bolivianos? It wouldn't be worth any more than that. I pay the best rates."

"You mean there are even bigger thieves than you! But that's not why I'm here. Boss, you ratted on that *chinita*."

Squinting frantically, whitey yelled, "I can't remember every single transaction! Get out! Come back when you're sober! I'll see if I can up my rate!"

"No, we'll settle this here and now. Boss, you informed on that *chinita* and now we need to have a little talk. Straight talk."

"Come back when you're not trashed."

"We're all mortal, boss, and at the worst your life is in no more danger than the light from that lamp. Boss, who put her in the can? Have you seen our empty shack? You will soon! Why haven't you opened the bag? Come on, Mr. Peredita, don't dillydally!"

"Okay, you stubborn drunk."

Casual as can be, honest whitey began to undo the bag: goat or pig who cares, but the boy's gnawed and severed head scared him out of his wits. "This is a crime! Do you want an alibi from me! Go away. I'm going to vomit! Go away. I won't tell anyone! Don't try to drag me into this, you monster! What can you give me? A handful of silver! A man in my position doesn't sell himself for nothing."

Zac's voice throbbed with anger: "That carcass is my son. Your fucking information put his mammy in the lockup. They left him by himself and the pigs ate him!"

"Idiot, don't try to charge this up to me. How horrible! How awful! I'm not to blame. I'll give you back your ring. I'll forget the bolivianos. You can brag you made a killing! Pick it all up. Give it a proper burial. I understand why you tried to drown your sorrows. Go! Go away. You can pick up the ring in the morning. And give those remains a decent burial."

"Don Quintito, you're coming with me, you bastard."

VIII

Scarface rears violently up on his steed, his lasso whips around terrified whitey's neck and whitey slumps to the ground, arms flailing.

The horse whirls around to a sound of crunching bone, bucks and crashes into the street, dragging whitey's body behind. Horseshoes glint; at the end of the rope, the limp body twists and turns. Bent low over the saddle, digging his spurs into his mount's flanks, the rider feels the rope tighten and the body drag as it bounces over the cobbles. Zac feels an Indian's stoic sadness and he feels consoled.

BOOK SEVEN

Necromancy

I

THE HORSES are ready for the great escape from Rancho Ticomaipú. Little Colonel de la Gándara is supping with Kid Filomeno. Nearing the end of the repast, the rancher orders young Laurita to bring the children. Resigned to the sad days ahead she goes to fetch them. Heedless of their mother, who glowers, pressing a finger to her lips, the kids rush into the room. The boss feels sorrow sapping his resolve. He stares at the tablecloth. Avoids the eyes of his wife and children. Finally looks up. He's got his grit back.

II

The kids stand silently in a circle of lamplight. Telepathic intuitions tremble in the air. "Children, I've worked hard to leave you land and property and spare you the path of the poor. It's a path I walked myself, and I didn't want you to. This determination has inspired my whole life—until today. Today has brought a change. My father left me no wealth, but he did leave me a name as honorable as any. And that is a legacy I want to pass down to you. I hope honor will mean more to you than all the gold in the world. I would be bitterly ashamed if it did not."

"Filomeno, you're always abandoning us!" groaned the lady of the ranch.

The boss's scowl shot that comment down. The eyes of his children moistened, but no tears fell. "I beg your mamma to be courageous and listen to what I have to say. As a good citizen, I worked for my family's well-being. I gave little thought to that of my fatherland, which demanded no sacrifice of me—until today. But today my conscience has wakened. I don't want to stand ashamed tomorrow or for you to stand ashamed of your father."

The lady of the ranch sobbed. "So you're going off to join that revolutionary rabble!"

"With my friend."

Little Colonel de la Gándara stood up and swaggered. He stretched out his arms. "You're a real Spartan noble! I'll never let you down!"

The rancher's wife sighed. "And if you die, Filomeno?"

"Be sure to bring up the children properly. They'll know that their father died for the fatherland."

Tumultuous images flashed through his wife's mind. Revolution. Death, arson, torture, and, far off, like an implacable deity, the mummified figure of Tyrant.

III

Scarface reined in his swift steed. A smell of basil came through the barred window. He'd raced there across pitch-dark fields. "Get your spurs on, Little Colonel! Whitey ratted on my wife, though I sure paid him back for his trouble. Get your spurs on!"

Zac brought his mount to a halt. His gloomy face and muted voice penetrated the iron bars. Everyone inside turned toward the grille. The colonel asked, "So what happened?"

"The blackest storm in my life. The glitter on that ring brought bad luck! Get your spurs on, Colonel, the dogs are yapping at my heels!"

IV

The lady of the ranch hugs her husband; the children huddle and whimper, clinging to their mother's skirts. Grandma from Rome rushes in. In a hoarse voice, she cries out, "Perché questa folia? Se il Filomeno trova fortuna nella rivoluzione potrá diventar un Garibaldi. Non mi spaventar i bambini!"

Scarface stared through the bars, his entire face in the shadows. Now and then his horse's huge eye caught the light of the chandelier and the shifting play of broken shadows in the room. Zac was still riding with the bag with his dead child on his saddle. The family gathered around the boss in the sitting room. One by one the mother pulled out a child for the father to hug. Zac was despondent. "They're bits of his heart."

V

Old China led up the horses. Soon the sound of their galloping echoed in the black night. They rode to a river and reined in their horses. Zac drew alongside the little colonel. "That bastard Banderitas is done for! We've got the best insurance. Riding here with me!"

The little colonel thought he must be drunk. "What's that, buddy?"

"My kid's remains. Relics. What was left after the pigs butchered him. Here in this bag."

The colonel held out his hand. "Zacarías, I am sorry. But why haven't you buried them?"

"In due time."

"It doesn't seem right to me."

"These relics are our passport."

"That's an old wives' tale!"

"Boss, that asshole whitey could tell you a thing or two!"

"What did you do?"

"I strung him up. What else could I do?"

"You have to bury him."

"When we're safe and sound."

"He was such a lively little kid!"

"You're telling me!"

PART FIVE

Santa Mónica

BOOK ONE

Seats in the Shade

I

GHASTLY legends of poisoned water, of snake-ridden dungeons, torturers' chains, racks, and hooks swathed the Fortress of Santa Mónica, home to countless political prisoners during revolutionary struggles. These legends went back to the time of Spanish rule and in the era of the tyrant General Santos Banderas they'd grown stronger. Every afternoon, to the sound of bugles, a bunch of revolutionaries met their death at Santa Mónica, sentenced not by law but on secret instructions from Tyrant.

II

Sandwiched between guards, Nachito and the student passed the postern gate. Del Valle had sent a sergeant from the canteen, and based on his verbal report the governor admitted them. As they walked through the gate, the two handcuffed men gazed at the remote, luminous blue of the sky. In chronicles of those times the governor of Santa Mónica, Colonel Irineo Castañon, crops up as one of Tyrant's cruelest killers—a bloodthirsty, grotesque, pipe-smoking old man hopping about on a peg leg. The colonel welcomed the two prisoners with cruel sarcasm, his flies unbuttoned: "I am so proud to welcome such very important people!"

Nachito flashed a fake smile. He decided to speak up for himself: "I'm sure there's been a grave error, Colonel."

The colonel emptied his pipe, knocking it against his peg leg.

"That's no concern of mine. Trials, when they take place, are the preserve of Attorney Carballeda. You are simply under arrest. The whole castle is yours!"

Nachito pretended to smile gratefully. He sniveled. "This is a total nightmare!"

Standing in the doorway the warder rattled his keys. He was a mulatto, thin as a rake, robotic in his movements. He wore a battered French kepi, colored military-issue trousers, and a very greasy Indian tunic. The patent leather was flaking off of his old shoes, and they cut into his bunions. The governor joked: "Don Trini, give these two front-row seats."

"They'll have no reason to complain. If they're just visiting, I'll give them sea views from the wall."

The prisoners were frisked, then Don Trini led them through a low vaulted passage lined with cupboards full of rifles. At the end he opened a barred door and let them loose under the fortress walls. "Walk as much as you like."

As always, Nachito fawned. "Thank you so much, Don Trini."

Unmoved, Don Trini slammed the door. Bolts and locks grated. As he walked away, he shouted, "There's a canteen, if you want something to eat or drink—and can pay."

III

Nachito sighed. He studied the prison walls emblazoned with graffiti of phallic spoils. Behind him a taciturn student rolled a cigarette. His eyes twinkled with amusement and he pursed lips that were as dark as blackberries. He was aloof yet compassionate. Some prisoners strolled about in miserable isolation. Down below waves swirled and crashed, as if to undermine the prison's foundations. Forests of nettles grew in shadowy corners. A flock of jet-black buzzards circled above in the blue sky. Nachito flexed his legs conceitedly and glanced at the student reproachfully. "You know, your silence is hardly cheering. It could even be seen as impolite. What's your name, friend?"

"Marco Aurelio."

"Marquito, what's going to happen to us?"

"How should I know?"

"It's frightening here! Listen to those lashing waves! It's like being on a boat."

The Fortress of Santa Mónica, a dramatic castle with defenses dating back to the viceroyalty, was built on coastal reefs above the vast equatorial sea, sinister in squalls and in lulls between squalls. A few ancient cannons, corroded by salt, lined the barbican, where prisoners' shirts hung out to dry. An old man sat on the parapet above the sea, mending a blanket. A cat hunted lizards on the highest rampart. Platoons of soldiers exercised at Snake Point.

IV

Corpses bobbed in the foaming waves lashing the fortress wall, their bloated bellies bruised black-and-blue. Clamoring mutinously, prisoners climbed the ramparts. The waves rocked the corpses and rolled them up against the prison wall. The blazing sky was home to mangy buzzards, hovering high in the cruelly indifferent turquoise. The prisoner who was mending his blanket broke his thread and held his needle to his fat lip. He muttered bitterly: "The fucking sharks are weary of all that revolutionary flesh, but that bastard Banderas still isn't satisfied! Hell!"

There was a stoic aspect to his wrinkled leathery face, and his long, ashen-gray beard made him look even more severe. Nachito and Marco Aurelio were hesitant, like travelers who have lost their way. Meeting a prisoner, Nachito gave way with a friendly smile. They reached the ramparts and leaned over to look at the sea, gleeful in the morning light, necromantic with bodies churning miserably in the foaming swell. Prisoners clambered on the walls, belting out mutinous songs, scowling angrily, and gesticulating. Nachito was shocked and frightened. Had the corpses washed up from some shipwreck?

The old man with the blanket gave him a withering look. "They're our people. They were killed in Foso-Palmitos."

"They didn't bury them?" the student asked.

"Are you kidding? They throw them into the sea, but the sharks are glutted on the flesh of revolutionaries, so they'll have to bury whoever's next in line."

He laughed bitterly. Nachito shut his eyes. "Friend, have you been sentenced to death?"

"Have you ever known the Tiger of Zamalpoa to issue a more lenient verdict? A death sentence! I'm not afraid and I'm not going anywhere! Down with Tyrant!"

Perched on the parapet, the prisoners gazed at the green swell churning against the ramparts. Shaking with fury, they roared out insults. Dr. Alfredo Sánchez Ocaña, poet and satirist, a famous tribune of the revolution, held one arm aloft and began a harangue. The ink-black eyes of the sentinel at the postern gate observed him. The sentinel held his rifle at the ready. "Heroes in the cause of freedom! Martyrs to the noblest of ideals! Your names, written in letters of gold, will emblazon the pages of our History! Brothers, we who are about to die salute you and give you our weapons!"

He swept off his hat and everyone followed suit. The sentinel cocked his rifle. "Get back! You're not allowed on the rampart."

Dr. Sánchez Ocaña cursed him: "You vile lackey!"

A coast guard boat lowered sail and maneuvered to salvage the corpses, landing seven. The prisoners refused to leave the ramparts. They began to riot. Guards ran out. Bugles blared.

V

Gripped by epileptic terror, Nachito grabbed the student's arm. "We're fucked!"

The old man with the blanket gave him a lingering glance. His fat lip trembled and he let out a goatish cackle. "This bastard of a life doesn't merit so much grief."

Nachito puled and whimpered. "It's so wretched to be innocent and to die! I am the victim of appearances. A terrible thing. I've been wrongly arrested!"

The old man's mocking mien turned to an insulting scowl. "Aren't you a revolutionary? At least you'll come to an honorable end, even if you don't deserve it."

Nachito relapsed into despair. He looked imploringly at the old man, who frowned and studied the geometric pattern of a patch on his blanket. Nachito tried to ingratiate himself with the weather-beaten veteran: chance had brought them together under the fig tree in the corner of that courtyard. "I have never supported the ideas behind the revolution. I deplore them. But I can understand you are heroes who have earned a place in history: Martyrs to an Idea. You know, my friend, Dr. Sánchez Ocaña is a brilliant speaker!"

The student concurred, somber yet passionate. "The best brains in the republic fight on the side of the revolution."

Nachito fawned: "The best!"

But the irritable old man kept stitching away at his blanket. He spoke with contempt. "It's plain there's nothing like a visit to Santa Mónica if you want to know what's happening. Seems like this young pup is no revolutionary either."

Marco Aurelio rose to the occasion. "I should have known better. I will be one, if I ever get out of here."

The old man knotted off a thread and laughed his goatish laugh. "The road to Hell is paved with good intentions."

Marco Aurelio looked at the old conspirator, and what he'd just said sounded so sensible to him that he wasn't outraged in the least. He sounded perfectly reasonable. His words were irrefutable in that jail crammed with political prisoners who were proud to die.

VI

The sea crashed against the fortress wall and the waves chorused a hymn to the victory of death. Black birds circled in the distant blue, and the shadows of their fluttering wings flickered over the flagstones in the courtyard. Marco Aurelio felt ashamed of the cosseted life he'd led, clinging to his mother's skirts, absurdly unaware, like a doll dropped after a tea party: he couldn't shake the remorse he felt for his lack of political commitment. Those walls, that prison stuffed with real-life revolutionaries, filled him with sorrow and with a sense of how petty his own existence was and how infantilized he'd been by his family and his studies, with nothing to show for himself except some laurels from the lecture hall. He was filled with shame as he hung on the words of the old man who went on plying his darning needle. "Have you come to this pit for respectable reasons, or are you a spy? That needs to be cleared up. See if you can find someone who will speak up for you. You say you're a student? Well, there's no lack of university folk here. If you want a friend here you need to justify your own presence. We don't trust armchair revolutionaries."

All color drained from the student's face. Nachito, doggy-eyed, sniveled for mercy. "I too am horrified by Tyrant Banderas. He's so bloodthirsty! But it wasn't easy to break the chain. I'm hopeless when it comes to fisticuffs, and completely hopeless when it comes to earning a living. The generalito gave me a bone to gnaw on. He had fun making fun of me. Deep down, I think he may even have a certain regard for me. Yes, yes, I was wrong, I'm a shit and it was all bullshit. Yes, human dignity has its claims. Yes, yes, yes. But please consider the situation of a man who, thanks to the inheritance laws, lacks any options. My dad was an alcoholic! My mom was crazy. A real madwoman! And though the generalito made fun of me, he still liked the silly things I said. People envied me. How the mighty are fallen!"

Marco Aurelio and the old conspirator listened silently, glancing at each other from time to time. The old man summed up: "Some people are lower than whores!"

Nachito choked. "That's the final straw! That's really beyond the pale. No one's ever said that to me. To take pleasure executing a wretched orphan is worthy of Nero. I'd be grateful to Marquito and to you, my friend, to put me out of my misery. Enough! What's the point of living a few more hours if sheer terror drains life of all pleasure! I know what lies in store for me, the Spirits warned me—yes, believe me, the Blessed Souls are behind this fracas. Marquito, go on, stick the knife in, twist it, spare me this nerve-racking torture. I renounce life. Old man, why don't you lance me with that darning needle? Thrust it into my heart! What do you say, friends? If you're afraid, at least try to make my lot easier."

VII

A mixture of pity and scorn marked the old man's death mask and the student's restless pallor as the two of them listened to the nincompoop gush pusillanimous pleas. The disgraced buffoon's meltdown reminded them of those grotesquely pompous burials that are put on at carnival to prepare the way for Lent. Buzzards on the fig tree flapped their scabby wings.

BOOK TWO

The Number Three

I

CELL NUMBER three was a former stable. Lamps behind bars set in the high ceiling brought a dim light to a place that stank of alcohol, sweat, and cigarettes. On each side of the room prisoners' hammocks hung in rows: most of them were politicals, though there was also space in that joint for the occasional gray-haired thief, bloodthirsty madman, stupid hothead, or spineless hypocrite. Since these fellows made life miserable for the politicals, Colonel Irineo Castañon, the man with the peg leg, enjoyed ditching them there. Dust-specked light slid down the dirty, whitewashed walls, desolate, arid, and a perfect match for the prisoners' emaciated features. Shirt cuffs flapping, arm defiantly raised, vituperative Dr. Sánchez Ocaña declaimed against tyranny: "The funereal phoenix of colonial absolutism rises anew from ashes cast to the four winds, summoning the shades and spirits of our illustrious liberators. They *were* illustrious, and their exemplary lives will enlighten these hours that may be our last. The sea returns its heroes to the land; the voracious monsters in the blue depths are more merciful than General Santos Banderas... Our eyes—"

He broke off. The peg leg approached along the passageway. The governor walked by, smoking his pipe. The warning tap of his limping gait faded away.

II

Lying in a hammock a prisoner pulled out the book he'd hidden away. From the adjacent hammock Don Roque Cepeda's shadowy form asked, "Still reading *Famous Escapes*?"

"One must study the classics."

"That book fascinates you. Are you dreaming of making an escape?"

"Well, who knows?"

"It would be good to get one over on Colonel Peg Leg!"

The reader sighed and closed his book. "It's not even worth thinking about. Most likely we'll be executed this very afternoon."

Don Roque shook his head, burning with conviction. "I don't know about you, but I'm sure that the revolution will triumph and I will see it triumph. Perhaps later it will cost me my life. Perhaps. There's no escaping fate."

"Any idea what fate has in store for you?"

"I'm not destined to die in Santa Mónica, I know. I'm half a century old and I've achieved nothing. I've been a dreamer all these years. I must be reborn as one who toils for the people's cause—and dies when the people are reborn."

He spoke with the feverish glow of a dying man receiving final sacraments, clinging for comfort to the afterlife. His face glowed, his hand on the pillow was that of a crude wooden saint, his torso swelled out under the shroud-like blanket: resurrection was already here. The other prisoner gave him a friendly, skeptical, somewhat mocking smile. "If only I shared your faith, Don Roque! But I'm afraid they'll execute us both in Foso-Palmitos."

"That will never be my fate. But stop this gloomy nonsense and go back to dreaming of escape."

"We're opposites. You sit waiting for some unknown force to open these bars. I plan my escape tirelessly, certain all the time that the end is nigh. Which is what keeps me going. To avoid total collapse, I keep an eye open for a lucky breakthrough that of course won't ever happen."

"We can defeat Destiny, if we know how to summon our spiritual energies to fight it. There are forces latent within us, powers beyond knowledge. Given your state of mind, I'd recommend reading something more spiritual than *Famous Escapes*. I'll get you *The Path of Theosophy*. It will reveal new, unknown horizons."

"Like I said, we are polar opposites. These esoteric authors of yours leave me cold. I guess I don't have a religious bent. That must be it. As far as I'm concerned, everything ends in Foso-Palmitos."

"But if you acquiesce in this lack of religious fever, you will prove a most mediocre revolutionary. You must believe that life is a holy seed given to us to nurture for the benefit of mankind. The revolutionary is a seer."

"I can accept that."

"And who gives us this existence with its specific burden of meaning? Who seals it with an obligation? Can we betray that with impunity? Can you really think there's no such thing as retribution?"

"After death?"

"After death."

"I don't try to resolve such matters."

"Perhaps you don't formulate them zealously enough."

"Perhaps."

"And doesn't the enigma of life obsess you?"

"I prefer not to think about it."

"And does that work?"

"So far, so good."

"And now?"

"Prisons are contagious places... If you keep talking in this vein, I'll end up saying the Creed."

"If I annoy you, I will forebear."

"Don Roque, I find pleasure in what you say, but your bouquet holds a thorn and the thorn pricks. Why do you believe my revolutionary actions will always be mediocre? What, in your view, is the relationship between religious awareness and political ideals?"

"My dear friend, they are one and the same!"

"One and the same? Possibly. I don't see it myself."

"Through profound contemplation you'll grasp many truths that can't be revealed otherwise."

"Each individual is a world unto himself, and we're just very different. Don Roque, you soar to great heights; me, I cling to the ground. But when you dub me a mediocre revolutionary, you're the one who's lost in the dark. Religion and our political struggles have nothing in common."

"The intuition of eternity marks every man. Only men who light their every step with its flame shall enter the annals of history. The intuition of eternity! This is religious consciousness, this is our burden as intellectuals! Its cornerstone is the redemption of the Indian, a profoundly Christian sentiment."

"Liberty, equality, and fraternity were, in my book, the touchstones of the French Revolution. Don Roque, we may be good friends, but we'll never agree on this one. Didn't the French Revolution preach atheism? Marat, Danton, Robespierre—"

"Profoundly religious spirits, although they may have preferred not to know."

"Blessed ignorance! Don Roque, grant me that and pluck out that thorn you stuck in my side."

"Granted. Please don't bear me any ill will."

They shook hands and fell silent, each reclining in his hammock. At the back of the gallery, Dr. Sánchez Ocaña went on haranguing a group of prisoners. The man's tropes and metaphors flowed freely, but his manner was frosty. In cell number three, reeking of sweat, booze, and tobacco, there was no mistaking that.

III

Don Roque Cepeda lay in his hammock surrounded by a group of adepts. Hope and optimism imbued his soft patter. He smiled a brightly seraphic smile. Don Roque was profoundly religious, his religion fashioned from mystical intuitions and Hindustani maxims. He lived in a state of red-hot bliss and his worldly pilgrimage presented him with arcane duties as inevitable as the stars' circuits overhead. A devotee of theosophy, he sought to forge a link with universal consciousness in the profoundest depths of his soul. In a burst of divine inspiration it had come to him that humanity was answerable for all its actions in eternity. For Don Roque, men were angels in exile: guilty of a crime in heaven, they paid for their theological guilt along paths of time that were paths in this world. Every step, every minute in human life provoked eternal reverberations sealed by death in a circle of infinite responsibilities. Souls, stripped of their terrestrial wrapping, acted out their mundane past in the limpid, hermetic vision of pure consciences. And this circle of eternal contemplation—whether full of joy or of pain—was the immutable grand finale of human destiny and the redemption of the exiled angel. A sacred number sealed the pilgrimage through the clay of human forms. Each life, even the humblest, created a world, and when it passed beneath the archway of death, cyclical consciousness of this creation took possession of the soul, and the soul, imprisoned at its center, became contemplative and still. Don Roque was a man who had read widely and disconcertingly, in ways that linked theosophy with the cabala, occultism, and the philosophy of Alexandria. He was on the cusp of fifty. He had the broad forehead and gleaming pate of a Romanesque saint, to which dark black eyebrows lent an austere energy. His body disclosed a sturdy skeleton and vibrated with the fortitude of the olive and the vine. His revolutionary preaching shone with the light of early-morning walks down hallowed paths.

BOOK THREE

Prison Pack

I

EIGHT or ten prisoners were playing cards in the light from a barred window. Chucho the Hobo shuffled: he was a thug, renowned for rustling, kidnapping wealthy landowners, holding up mail coaches, wreaking havoc, and petty crimes of all sorts; also for his cursing, his gangster's swagger, his love life, and his bloodthirsty jealousy. His lean hands shuffled slowly; there was a knife scar on his cheek and he was missing three teeth. Jailbirds of a very different stripe were also in the game: down-and-outs and doctors, guerrilla fighters and night watchmen had all gathered around to bet. Nachito Veguillas was around: he hadn't joined in the game yet, but he was keeping an eye on the pack while he fingered the money in his pocket. A jack turned up and he exclaimed ecstatically, "Got it right again!"

He swiveled around and smiled at the hesitant, deadpan gambler at his side: a specter in a flaccid drill jacket that hung from him as if from a meat hook. Nachito focused on the cards again. On an impulse he produced a fistful of sols and threw them down on the flea-bitten blanket that serves for green baize in a jail. "Ten sols on the fucking king."

Chucho the Hobo signaled. "You've just doubled the stake."

"Cut."

"Here we go!"

Hobo cut the pack and the king of clubs tumbled out. Nachito was thrilled to have won and went back for more. From time to time violent arguments broke out. Nachito beamed like a saint as he kept on winning; the hesitant, jaundiced specter wore a tight smile, which soon turned to an ominous scowl. Nachito returned his stare. Now his grieving heart cried out. "What does it matter if we win or lose? Foso-Palmitos levels all."

The other guy disagreed, hissing biliously like a punctured bladder. "While there's life, there's brass. That's all that counts. And don't you forget it!"

Nachito sighed. "If you're on death row, what consolation can money bring?"

"Well, at least gambling helps you forget... And money counts to the very end."

"My friend, are you also under sentence of death?"

"Who knows?"

"Won't they kill us all?"

"Who knows?"

"It's a ray of light! I'm betting fifty sols on the fourth cut."

Nachito won, and the other guy's pallid face wrinkled up. "Are you always on a winning streak?"

"I'm not complaining."

"How about a two-way five-sol stake? You play it your way."

"Five bets."

"Whatever."

"Let's go for the jack."

"You seem to like that card."

"It's all a crapshoot."

"It's going to break us."

"We'll see."

Chucho the Hobo shuffled slowly, then cut the deck so everyone could see; he kept his hand in the air for a moment. Out came the jack. Nachito raked in his winnings and split the column of sols into two, whispering to his yellow partner, "What did I tell you?"

"It's as if you can see through the cards!"

"Now we'll switch to number seven."

"What's your system?"

"'Love you; love you not.' I bet on a card I like, and then I bet on a card I don't like. Now I'm betting on the seven. I don't like seven."

"First time I've heard of that system: 'Love you; Love you not'!"

"I just invented it."

"We're gonna lose."

"Look, it's a seven."

"I've never seen such a run of luck!"

"Let's put our third bet on the queen."

"You like the queen?"

"No, I'm just grateful. Look, we've won! Time to divide the spoils."

"We said five bets."

"We'll lose."

"Or win. The 'love you' card is the five, now it's the turn of the 'love you not' card."

"This is risky business! Let's hold on to half of our kitty."

"No, I'm keeping nothing back. Eighty sols on the three."

"It's not going to work this time."

"Can't always win."

"You can opt out."

Chucho the Hobo, keeping one eye on the pack, sized up the difference between the two cards at the top. He whistled contemptuously. "Wow wee ... Same difference."

He put the pack on the blanket and wiped his brow with a handsome silk handkerchief. He could see the gamblers were on tenterhooks. Scowling sarcastically, his scarred face all twisted up, he began to shuffle. Out came the number three. The specter at his side was shaking. "We've won!"

Nachito rapped his knuckles on the cloth and demanded the winnings: "One hundred and sixty sols."

Chucho the Hobo gave him a hard look and jeered as he paid up. "With your kind of luck, only a son of a bitch would have stayed in the game. It's like there's an angel whispering in your ear!"

Nachito nodded good-humoredly, stacked his money, and gave thanks: "Croak! Croak!"

And a captain named Viguri muttered churlishly, "The Virgin always appears to shepherds!"

At that very moment the jaundiced specter was whispering in Nachito's ear: "Time to split the takings."

Nachito shook his head, and his jaw hung open. "After the fifth bet."

"That's crazy."

"If we lose, we'll win another way. Who knows? Perhaps they won't execute us! And if we win, we'll get our comeuppance in Foso-Palmitos."

"Stuff it, friend. Don't tempt fate."

"Let's go for the jack again."

"An ill-omened card."

"So, it'll be the death of us. Hey you, Mr. Shuffle! That's a hundred and sixty on the jack."

The Hobo replied, "Done!"

Nachito fawned back: "Thank you kindly."

And the cardsharp retorted: "This'll be the death of *me*!"

He cut the pack and out strolled the jack, and the whole table murmured. Nachito turned pale, his hands shaking. "I'd have preferred to lose that one. Sorry, friend, we'll get our comeuppance in Foso-Palmitos!"

The specter's wan features brightened. "For the moment, let's just collect."

"That's one hundred and twenty-seven sols each."

"The cut has fucked us up."

"It could have fucked us up worse. In this kind of situation, it's bad luck to win at cards."

"Let Chucho keep the money then."

"That's hardly a solution."

"Are you going to go on playing?"

"Until I lose! That's the only way I can calm down."

"Well, I'm going to get some fresh air. Thanks for your help. Consider me a friend: Bernardino Arias."

He left. With trembling hands, Nachito stacked up his winnings.

Such ridiculous good luck boded ill. He would die. He was full of terror and anguish. Invisible forces had him at their mercy. They were circling around, hostile and mocking. He grabbed a handful of cash and put it on the first card to be dealt. He wanted to win and he wanted to lose. He shut his eyes, then opened them. Chucho the Hobo turned the pack over, shuffled and cut. Nachito was appalled. Once again he'd won. He smiled apologetically, under the crooked cardsharp's glare. "Well, they'll probably shoot me this afternoon!"

II

At the other end of the cell, some prisoners were listening to a one-eyed soldier tell a tale full of sibilant *s*'s and liquid *l*'s. He spoke in a monotone, sitting on his heels, as he related the defeat of revolutionary troops in Curopaitito. Five prisoners were sprawled on the ground in front of him. "When that happened, I was still with Doroteo Rojas's band. Life was lousy, I was wet through and through all the time, with my trigger finger itching. The blackest day was July 7: we were crossing a swamp when the *federales* started firing: we hadn't seen them because they were hidden behind some of those thorn bushes that were everywhere, and it was only by God's grace that we got out of that quagmire. The minute we were out, we returned fire mercilessly, but the exchange didn't let up, after which we were leg-leg-legging it over never-ending plains. A blistering sun turned the sand red-hot and us still leg-leg-legging it. We slunk off like coyotes, crawling through the mud, with the *federales* behind us. And the bullets kept winging past. And us still leg-leg-legging it all the time."

The Indian's voice, with its sibilant *s*'s and liquid *l*'s, seemed stuck on a single note. A famous orator on the revolutionary side, who'd been locked up for long months on end, a young man with a pale brow and a romantic sweep of hair, Dr. Atle sat up in his hammock and listened to the tale with rapt attention. Occasionally he jotted something down in his notebook. It seemed like the Indian was trying to lull himself to sleep with his monotonous patter. "Leg-leg-legging it all day until at dusk we spotted a shack that had been torched and rushed in for cover. But that didn't work. They drove us out, and we took shelter behind a waterwheel, but then they were firing again, bullets coming fierce and thick as hail until the ground began to boil. The *federales* had decided to finish us off. There were guns blazing, and soon all you could hear was zing, crackle, zing like when Mamma made popcorn. The friend at my side was dancing all over the place, so I said, 'Don't try and dodge the bullets, pal; it only makes it worse.' Then one smashed his head in and there he was, staring at the stars. At dawn we reached the foothills but there was no water, no corn, nothing to eat."

The Indian fell silent. The prisoners around him went on smoking impassively, as if they hadn't even heard. Dr. Atle perused his notes. Pencil on lip, he asked the soldier, "What is your name?"

"Indalecio."

"Surname?"

"Santana."

"Where are you from?"

"I was born on the Chamulpa estate. I was born there but when I was a kid they took me with a bunch of peons to a mine owned by some miserly whitey in the Llanos de Zamalpoa. When the revolution broke out, we all deserted and joined Doroteo's band."

Dr. Atle scribbled a few lines in his notebook, and then leaned back in his hammock, eyes closed, the pencil over his lips setting the seal on his sour features.

III

As the day advanced, the sun slanting through the high bars divided the whole cell into triangles of light and shadow. At that hour the odor of cigarettes and bodies grew thick and sticky. The prisoners were mostly dozing on their hammocks; whenever they turned over, the flies rose up, then settled back down again. Other prisoners huddled silently in triangles of darkness they had sought out. Conversation was reduced to a few words. Everyone knew what fate held in store: their wanderings in this world soon would be over and that insistent, torturing thought also engendered a stoic calm. Those brief conversations, conducted in the cheery light of lamps that were about to sputter out for lack of oil, brought back memories of long-forgotten smiles. Mortality gave an air of indulgent melancholy to eyes that were turning away from the world and looking back into the past. Sharing a destiny gave the same expression to different faces. Everyone felt transported to a distant shore, and the triangles of light slanting across the cell sharpened the silhouettes of those emaciated figures in modern, cubist style.

PART SIX

Honey-Nut Tarts and Poison

BOOK ONE

Loyola's Lesson

I

THE SAD Indian tries to forget his troubles with fighting cocks. In dives and bars he whispers about Kid Santos's injustice, cruelty, and magic powers. Saint Michael's Dragon had given the Kid secret spells. He was an initiate. Yes, they were buddies! They'd done a deal! Generalito Banderas had said that bullets couldn't harm him, a deal signed by Satan! Overshadowed by that invisible, vigilant presence, the coppery populace faced a religious destiny full of fear. Pure theological terror.

II

It was the changing of the guards in Saint-Martin of the Mostenses. The servile sweeney was soaping Tyrant's face. Major del Valle stood to attention, motionless in the doorway. Tyrant had heard his report, his back turned, deadpan, with a knowing look. "Our Master Veguillas is an innocent soul. A good mopping-up exercise, Major del Valle! You deserve a medal."

That insidious sarcasm didn't augur well. The major sensed the angry quivering of his lips. He instinctively exchanged glances with the aides, who were skulking in the background, a pair of young Turks in glittering uniforms, aiguillettes, and plumes. The room was a large, airy cell, with a dusty red floor and pigeons nesting in the beams. Tyrant Banderas turned around, his mask lathered in shaving soap. The major stood stiffly to attention in the doorway, his hand by his temples. He had decided four drinks would give him the Dutch courage to present his report and now felt distressingly unreal. The faces present looked distant, hesitant. There was a hazy sensation of nightmarish unreality. Tyrant stared at him silently, pursing his lips, then gestured to his servant to go on shaving. Don Cruz, the barber, was a spindly, elderly Negro, monkey-faced under graying frizz. Born into slavery, he wore the bedraggled, crestfallen look of a whipped dog. The fawning sweeney tiptoed around Tyrant. "How are the blades, boss?"

"Fit to shave the dead."

"But it's English steel!"

"Don Cruz, that must mean they haven't been properly sharpened."

"Boss, the red-hot sun in these parts has made your skin too sensitive."

The major stiffened in his military salute. Glancing at the little mirror opposite, Kid Santos saw the doorway and part of the room in distorted perspective. "I'm annoyed that Colonel de la Gándara has put himself outside the law. I'm so sorry to lose a friend. That hasty temper of his will be his ruin! I would like to have pardoned him, but our dear Master V has made it impossible. He's a soft-bellied soul. He can't bear upsets and he deserves a different sort of decoration: a cross with a pension. Major del Valle, prepare a summons for that ingenuous soul. By the way, why was the young student imprisoned?"

Standing to attention on the doorstep, Major del Valle tried to enlighten him. "We received a bad report and, well, that open window does not speak in his favor."

The major's voice has an opaque, mechanical ring, as if coming from miles away. Tyrant Banderas pursed his lips. "Nicely observed, especially since you were scared stiff at the sight of the roof below. And the boy's family—what's it like?"

"Son of the late Dr. Rosales."

"Hmmm. Have his utopian revolutionary sympathies been fully investigated? We need the police department's report. See to it, Major del Valle. Lieutenant Morcillo, issue orders for the immediate arrest of Colonel de la Gándara. Have the garrison commander dispatch forces to search the whole area. We must be quick. If we don't catch the little colonel now, he'll join the insurgents tomorrow. Lieutenant Valdivia, see if there's a long line for today's audiences."

The fawning sweeney finished shaving Tyrant and helped him into his clerical frock coat. Like German automata the aides swung halfway around and marched out of the room from opposite sides. They sheathed their sabers and clicked their spurs. "Chop-chop!"

The sun glinted on Tyrant's skull as he peered through the windowpanes. Bugles blared, and on the barren plot in front of the monastery, dragoons rode their horses round and round the mule-powered landau—a museum piece—that Kid Santos used for his state visits.

III

Tyrant Banderas scurried into the audience hall like a snoopy rat, buttoning up his clerical frock coat. "Salutem plurimam!"

Doña Rosita Pintado threw her shawl aside and hurled herself histrionically at the feet of Tyrant. "Generalito, what they're doing to my little boy is not right!"

The wizened Indian mummy frowned. "Arise, Doña Rosita. An audience with the nation's premier lawmaker is not a vaudeville show. What's wrong with the son of the late, lamented Dr. Rosales? That formidable patriot would have been most valuable in maintaining order today! Doña Rosita, what's your complaint?"

"Generalito, they took my boy off to prison this morning!"

"Doña Rosita, under what circumstances was he arrested?"

"Major del Valle was in hot pursuit of a fugitive."

"Had you given him shelter?"

"Of course not. It was your buddy Domiciano."

"My buddy Domiciano! Doña Rosita, you mean to say Colonel Domiciano de la Gándara?"

"You're a tyrant for correct titles!"

"Doña Rosita, the premier lawmaker of this land has no *buddies*. And how was it that little Colonel de la Gándara was visiting *you* at such an unlikely hour?"

"It went by like a flash, General! He ran in from the street and flew out the window without a single word."

"And how was it that it happened to be *your* house, Doña Rosita, that he chose?"

"Generalito, fate rules our lives. How should I know?"

"By the same token, you must wait to know your boy's fate. Which will be determined, of course, according to the laws of nature. My dear Madame Doña Rosita, I'm so very obliged to you for your visit. It's been such a pleasure to see you and recall those old times when the late, lamented Laurencio Rosales was courting you. I'll always remember you riding in that procession at Rancho el Talapachi! Console yourself that individually we have no power to alter our fate: yes, there's next to nothing we can do."

"Generalito, don't speak in riddles!"

"Just consider this for a second. Colonel de la Gándara escapes the law by jumping out of a window. Thus he opens a case that we have no choice now but to investigate. And that's where we stand. Madame Doña Rosita, let us agree that in this world we are merely rebellious children, walking with hands tied, forever subject to time's lash. But how is it, as I asked, that Colonel de la Gándara chose *your* house? Doña Rosita, I apologize for not giving you a longer audience. Be assured that justice will be done. And in the last instance, fate calls the shots! Be seeing you!"

Stiff as an iron rod he stepped back, gesturing sharply to an aide who stood to attention in the doorway. "That's it for today. We're off to Santa Mónica!"

IV

The sun's flame lit up the rugged stretch of roof terraces, a battlement blazing above the harbor's curve. Sinister in storms and lulls between storms, the vast equatorial sea lay still in sheets of light from closest quay to remotest horizon. Barbicans and ramparts reflected the rough hand of military geometry like bulldogs transmuted into mathematical formula. In the parade-ground bandstand a raucous combo of virtuosos entertained a local crowd. The strident brass was an insult to the silent desolation of a sky tortured by light. The rabble of blanketed Indians, skulking on sidewalks and along arcades or thronging the steps of churches and monasteries, genuflected to the passing Tyrant. The frock-coated mummy gave an amused wave. "Chop-chop! They look so submissive and yet it's impossible to govern them! Scholars are absolutely right when they tell us that Spanish individualism has eradicated the Indian's primitive communism. That's why we long for dictators. Creole dictators, apathetic natives, half-breed crooks, colonial theocracy! These are commonplaces that Yankee industrialists and European diplomats employ to put us down. They back the buccaneers of revolution so as to destroy our values and acquire our mines, railways, and customs taxes... Let's give them a real scare. We'll release the future president of the republic from prison with full honors!"

The generalito's ivories flashed a feigned smile. His aides nodded with military precision. With imperious glints and martial clatter, an escort of dragoons surrounded the landau. The rabble moved aside for fear of being trampled, and suddenly the street became an empty, silent, forlorn space. On the edge of the sidewalk, the shabby Indian in blanket and palm-frond hat knelt and waved religious crosses. Clapping and cheering enthusiastically, pool players peered over the balcony of the Spanish casino. The frocked mummy responded as decorously as a Quaker, raising his silk hat while his aides gave a military salute.

V

The Fortress of Santa Mónica rose above the luminous seashore like a melodrama in stone. The reserve corps stood at attention by the postern gate. Not a single wrinkle creased Tyrant's Indian mask as Colonel Irineo Castañon, Peg Leg, came forward to greet him. Tyrant's expression was carved in hard ridges like an obsidian idol's. "Where's Don Roque Cepeda?"

"Cell number three."

"I hope that distinguished patrician and his colleagues have been treated with consideration. Political opposition within the framework of the law merits all due respect from the institutions of the state. The rigor of the law must be applied to armed insurgents. From now on be sure to abide by these guidelines. It is our wish to meet the candidate of the opposition for the presidency of the republic. Colonel Castañon, at ease."

The colonel swiveled around, his hand raised to his cap in salute, his peg leg describing a stiff half circle through the air. He stopped and hopped and rasped bellicosely at the flunky with a bunch of keys: "Don Trinidad, you go!"

Don Trinidad trotted off, only delayed by his bunions. Bolts and hinges creaked. Once the spiked steel door opened, he cantered away, keys clinking and tinkling. A sprightly fellow, he bounced and pirouetted (in beat-up deluxe patent leathers), while Colonel Irineo Castañon marked time. Tap! Tap! The tripping rhythm of his peg leg echoed through the vaults and galleries. Tap! Tap! Foxy and sanctimonious, Tyrant, surrounded by grinning aides, wrinkled his lips. Colonel Alcaide panted breathlessly. "Cell number three!"

On the threshold, Tyrant Banderas doffed his hat in greeting and peered inside looking for Don Roque. The entire prison was standing around the door, silent and on tenterhooks. Accustomed now to the cell's dim light, Tyrant strode between the two rows of hammocks. He clung to his ancient rituals, deferentially greeting the circle around Don Roque. "My dear sir, Don Roque, I have only just been informed of your detention in this fortress. I deplore this situation! Please do me the honor of believing that it is none of my doing. Santos Banderas has great regard for such an esteemed member of the republic as yourself, and our ideological differences may not be as irreducible as you suppose, my dear Don Roque. Though you purport to be my adversary in politics, you act at all times like one who is conscious of his civic duties. You participate in the primaries. Your battles are conducted within the charter of the constitution. My rule has been renowned for the severe rulings issued by our judges against provocateurs who take up arms and act outside the law. I shall always be merciless against such tin-pot warriors who are keen only to spark foreign intervention, but I shall always respect and even commend that opposition which operates strictly according to the laws of the land. Don Roque, that's where you come in. Right off I want to say that I fully acknowledge your patriotism and appreciate the generous intentions behind your campaign to imbue the indigenous race with civic spirit. This matter needs to be debated, but for the moment I wish merely to offer my apologies for this regrettable police error by which a good man has, as Horace puts it, come to dignify the prison house of vice and of corruption."

Silent and incredulous, Don Roque's friends had circled around. Now Don Roque broke into a smile, a rustic saint's smile that rippled gently over his bronze face. "General, sir, excuse me for being blunt. When I listen to you I think I must be listening to the Serpent in Genesis."

The expression in his eyes and his rippling smile and wrinkles looked so honest and innocent they gave his less than approving comment a benevolent tone. The furrows in Tyrant Banderas's green grimace froze in place. "Don Roque, I wasn't expecting such an insinuation. I only wanted to offer my loyal friendship and shake your hand, but as you believe me to be insincere, I can only reiterate my apologies."

He bid farewell with a sweep of his top hat and, flanked by his aides, headed for the door.

VI

Master Veguillas jumped down between the double row of hammocks, whimpering grotesquely, "Croak! Croak!"

The mummy pursed his lips. "Idiot!"

"Croak! Croak!"

"Don't clown."

"Croak! Croak!"

"Your japing isn't exactly amusing right now."

"Croak! Croak!"

"I'll have to kick you out of my way. With the toe of my boot!"

"Croak! Croak!"

Master V pulled in his guayabera and hopped on his haunches, whimpering, his face bloated, his eyes imploring.

"You're embarrassing! That froggy chorus doesn't make up for your crimes."

"My Generalito is a mine of magnetic contradictions."

Tyrant Banderas kicked him with the toe of his boot in front of the guard, who was presenting arms in the doorway. "I'll give you a jester's jingle-jangle hat."

"Why bother, my Generalito!"

"So you can take yourself and it to Saint Peter. Get a move on. I'll give you a ride in my carriage to the Mostenses. I don't want you going into the next world with any bad feelings for Santos Banderas. Come, let us converse, since the day will soon come when all conversation must cease. You may receive a death sentence, Master V. Why did you behave like such a skunk? Who persuaded you to divulge the president's decisions? What motivated these objectionable acts? Who are your accomplices? Do me the honor of climbing into my carriage. Sit next to me. You haven't been formally indicted by the court as yet. Far be it from me to anticipate your delinquency."

BOOK TWO

Human Frailty

I

DON MARIANO Isabel Cristino Queralt y Roca de Togores, His Catholic Majesty's plenipotentiary minister in Santa Fe de Tierra Firme, Baron of Benicarlés and Master Chevalier of Ronda, more beribboned than a Gypsy ass, was in bed at midday, wearing a lace cap and a pink silk dressing gown. Merlin, his toy terrier, licked his powdered face, smearing the rouge around with his spatula of a tongue. The drooling doggy's snout kneaded, caressed, and frotted his daddy.

II

Unannounced by his page, Currito My-Cutie gamboled in. The Andalusian boy stopped in the doorway, his nails drumming on the large brim of his Cordoban hat before sending it flying sideways. The youngster from the valleys accompanied that deft gesture with a deep-throated song, warbled in the best style of Sevillian *cante*, "Guy! You all ready for some Easter Passion? Merlin's made you look exactly like a flagellant."

His Excellency rolled over, turning his back on the bumptious boy. "You are *incorrigible*! Yesterday, I didn't see you for one measly second."

"Lodge a diplomatic complaint. I'm just out of the jug, as we jailbirds like to say."

"Cut the wisecracks, Curro. We are not amused."

"Oh, you don't say, Isabelita."

"You are *incorrigible*! You got yourself into a tight corner?"

"Victim of a grudge. I slept in the slammer, on a mat, and that's not the worst of it. The cops snatched all my business and correspondence."

Spain's minister sat up on his pillows, grabbed his lapdog by the curls on its neck, and splattered it on the carpet. "What did you say?"

Curro looked pained. "Isabelita, a poultice for its wick!"

"Where did you keep my letters?"

"In a case with seven spring-action padlocks."

"I know you, Curro! You dreamed all this nonsense up in order to extract some cash from me."

"It's not a squeeze, Isabelita!"

"Curro, you are *shameless*!"

"Isabelita, darling, thanks for the compliment, but the Honorable López de Salamanca has a monopoly in that particular bullfight."

"Currito, you're a bastard!"

"If only a bull *would* come and gore me!"

"Letters like that are burned! It's only proper!"

"But one *always* keeps them."

"The president's stuck his oar in! I'd rather not think about it. The situation is difficult. Indeed charged."

"Not the first time for you, I bet!"

"Don't tease! As things stand it may cost me my post."

"Parry and feint!"

"I'm not that tight with the government."

"Well, hide behind a big bull and wave your red cape. I'm sure that's not too much for you, sweetie!"

His Catholic Majesty's representative stuck his feet out of bed and put his head in his hands. "If this reaches the newspapers, I'll be in an impossible position! It will cost me an arm and a leg to keep them quiet!"

"Pull the wool over Tyrant's eyes."

Spain's minister stood up, clenching his fists. "I don't know why I don't scratch your eyes out!"

"Your self-restraint is much appreciated."

"You are a bastard, Currito. These are cunning ploys to wheedle money out of me. It's torture, plain and simple."

"Isabelita, see these crucifixes? I swear by all that's most holy you've got it wrong."

The baron was afraid. "You bastard!"

"Stop that refrain. I swear by the scapulary my poor mother wrapped around me when I sailed from my beloved Spain."

Curro softened at that echo of a sentimental Andalusian ballad. His Excellency's bulging far-focused blue eyes glittered ironically. "Well, you can be my handmaiden."

"So, who's being *shameless* now?"

III

Perfumed and spruced up, his Catholic Majesty's representative walked into the drawing room where Don Celes was waiting. Sensually decadent pessimism, nourished by literary airs, had turned up a new shade of rouge to revivify the diplomatic roué's psychological state. Reeling from the bitter aftertaste of love, he would sublimate the dregs of his conscience with nods to the eternal classics. When in society, he knew how to pass off his abhorrent tastes with the easy-going cynicism of a Beau Brummel from Bath. He always had an epigram ready to amuse bemused young colleagues who seemed so bereft of imagination and humanistic culture. He would insinuate indiscreetly that he was a high priest of both Hebe and Ganymede, allowing his vanity and deceitfulness to thrive behind a façade of frivolous libertinage, since he was careful not to sacrifice Hebe. By flirting with the ladies and engaging in vacuous, whispered gossip larded with teasing tittle-tattle, the Baron of Benicarlés cultivated countless skin-deep connections. The ladies were wooed by his dinner-jacketed, diplomatic ennui, those rhetorical flourishes gloved in London, laced with witty one-liners and embroidered by gold-capped smiles. How those autumnal hens clucked at his barbed darts. Shouldn't the world make us a little more comfortable, given we'd taken the trouble to pay it a visit? Wouldn't it be just divine if there were fewer fools to deal with, if toothache didn't exist and the bankers canceled our debts? Everybody should have to die at the same time, like military call-up. These are pressing reforms, but the Great Architect is not up-to-date with the current technology. Yankee and German industrialists need to be brought onto the boards of directors; they'd know how to improve the state of the world. His Catholic Majesty's minister's intellect was highly prized in that circle of ladies, though they sought in vain to tempt him with tender looks.

IV

"My dear Celes!"

As he entered the drawing room, a blubbery smile concealed an anguished heart, embossed with fear: Don Celes! Those letters! Tyrant's grimace! The roué netted that triad in a circumflex of thought, as he recalled his amorous epistles and the sorrow and pain and disgust he had endured in a distant European court. Distinguished whitey stood in the lounge, his Panama hat and gloves resting on his jutting paunch. Pompous and paltry, his hand outstretched as he stepped forward out of a frame of gilt, he halted, terrified by the yapping lapdog that was extracting his pointed snout from between His Excellency's shanks, as fussy and frosty as ever. "He refuses to see me as a friend."

As if offering his condolences, Don Celes shook the roué's hand in a leisurely way. He felt a surge of benign indifference.

"My dear Celes, your face is the harbinger of headline news!"

"My dear friend, I am sad."

The Baron of Benicarlés grinned like a harlot and asked, "What's up?"

"Dear Mariano, it is deeply mortifying to have to take this step. Believe me. But given the critical condition of the country's finances, my only option is to pursue liquidity."

His Catholic Majesty's minister continued to shake distinguished whitey's hands, oozing hypocritically, "Celes, you're the finest man I know. I can see how it pains you to ask me for your money back. Today you've shown incredible generosity. Have you heard the news from Spain?"

"Is there a packet in port?"

"I speak of a telegram."

"Political changes?"

"The pragmatists are at the palace gates."

"Indeed? That's no surprise. I'd heard as much, but it's simply a shotgun marriage."

"Celes, you'll be the next minister of the exchequer. Don't forget your exiled friend and give me a hug."

"Dear Mariano!"

"How you deserve this triumph, Celestino!"

The smarmy hypocrite led the pompous plutocrat over to sit on a sofa, and, sashaying his hips, settled down at his side. Whitey's paunch swelled with self-satisfaction. Prime Minister Emilio Castelar would wire his appointment. The mother country! He had but a faint inkling of his new duties but already he was preening: an adipose pillar of society. He had a strange sensation: his shadow seemed to be expanding exponentially, while his body shrank. He softened. His ears resounded with primordial words—Elevation, White Paper, Parliament, Sacrifice. And he embraced a theme: "Everything for the mother country!" That flabby femme, with her tiara, buckler, and rapier, enraptured him like a leading lady lurking in the wings before tripping out into the spotlights. Don Celes felt himself transported by haughty breezes blowing down the corridors of power, and yet he envisioned his fate as a minister with some apprehension. There he was, in his ceremonial, embroidered frock coat, spraying out his feathers like a fairytale peacock, but financial caution hedged that fond fancying with the arabesques of ominous fugues. Distinguished whitey was afraid his capital might plunge if he swapped exploiting Indians and blacks for serving the mother country. He patted his chest and extracted his wallet. "My dear Mariano, really and truly, in the circumstances that presently afflict this country and given its rocky finances, to uproot myself and go to Spain would be too much of a shock! You know me, you know how it irks me to put pressure on you, you recognize my good intentions, so I hope you won't do anything embarrassing."

The Baron of Benicarlés manufactured a thin smile and tweaked Merlin's ears. "Why, dearest Celestino, you're saying *my* part! I wholly accept your apologies. No need for you to say anything more. And your wallet, dearest Celestino, is more frightening to me than any pistol! Put it away and let's talk some more! I've got a farmhouse for sale in Alicante. Why don't you buy it? It would be a splendid gift for your friend, that eloquent tribune, our new prime minister. Buy it. I'll give it to you cheap."

Don Celes Galindo half closed his eyed, smiling like the Delphic oracle between his ginger whiskers.

V

The volutes of distinguished whitey's thoughts twisted high up into the vaulted limbo. A devotee of tradition, presumptuous and aggrieved, he considered His Catholic Majesty's minister's epistles to the Sevillian Currito a scandal to the red and gold of the nation's flag. Abominations! But now he had a sudden vision of Tyrant Banderas grimacing in his silent, shadowy tower. Abominations! His green grimace was shredding letters. And now Don Celes pledged himself to the mother country, a favored son offering his blushing, bulging baldpate on a sacrificial tray. Just as blood rushes gloriously to the cheeks when a toast is raised to the nation, he was full of a warm, generous determination to cover up any exposed privates with a fig leaf. The plump plutocrat quivered magnanimously. The baron shifted uncomfortably on the sofa, and an ambiguous, honeyed pro forma smile spread across his face. Don Celestino stretched out a sorrowful, pious hand, like María Verónica in the Way of the Cross painting. "I have lived long. When one has lived long, one acquires a modicum of insight into human behavior. You take my drift, dear Mariano?"

"Not yet."

The Baron of Benicarlés's eyelids slipped down, curtailing the blue horizons of his bulging eyes. Don Celes's face assumed an overwhelmingly confiding look. "Yesterday, the gendarmes, exceeding their powers in my opinion, arrested a Spanish subject and searched his suitcases... In my opinion, as I said, overstepping their powers."

The diplomatic roué nodded prudishly. "So I just learned. Currito My-Cutie paid me a visit and told me the sad news."

His Catholic Majesty's minister smiled, and the mask of rouge on his smooth cheeks began to crack, sarcastic like a wrinkled Venetian domino. Don Celes voiced his worries: "Mariano, this is deeply troubling. You will agree, this must be kept silent."

"My dearest Celestino, you're an innocent abroad! It's all quite trivial."

As his mask shrank, the rouge fissured even further and Don Celes became even more overbearing. "Dear Mariano, it is my duty to forewarn you. Those letters are now in the possession of General Banderas. Perhaps they contain some political secret, or a betrayal of your friendship—and the fatherland! Dear Mariano, we cannot, must not, forget the fatherland in all this! Those letters are in the hands of General Banderas."

"How gratifying. The president will be sure to take good care of them."

The Baron of Benicarlés retreated into the sibylline stance of a subtly perverse hierophant. Don Celes persisted, with added emphasis: "Mariano, as I said, I do not wish to prejudge those letters, but it *is* my duty to forewarn you."

"And I thank you for your pains. My distinguished friend, you let your imagination run riot. Believe me, those letters are quite trivial."

"I'd be very happy if that was so. But I'm afraid of scandal, dear Mariano."

"Are things here so uncivilized? It would be the height of absurdity."

Don Celes concurred, underlining his agreement with a wave of his hand. "No doubt, but we must silence any scandal."

The Baron of Benicarlés half closed his eyes and spoke with contempt: "Simply a little lunacy on the side. I do confess to finding Currito quite charming. Don't you know him? It might be worth your while!"

He smiled so pleasantly as he spoke, adding a touch of elegant English phlegm, that astonished whitey couldn't bring himself to pull out all the stops. Instead he muttered and fidgeted with his gloves. "No, I don't know him. Mariano, my advice to you is to keep on the right side of the general."

"Don't you think I am?"

"I think you should go see him."

"Why of course."

"Mariano, go, I beg you, on behalf of the mother country. For her sake and for the colony's. You know how the colony contains many illiterates without sophistication or culture. If the telegram brings fresh political news—"

"I'll keep you posted and, once again, my congratulations. Plutarch would have adored you. Goodbye, dear Celes."

"Go see the president."

"I will. This very afternoon."

"I leave reassured now that I have received your pledge."

VI

Currito My-Cutie sprang out from behind the curtains and, as he would have put it, was perkier than a cat that's got into the cream. "Oh, you were wonderful, Isabelita!"

With a regal flourish the Baron of Benicarlés cut him dead. Flushed, in deep dudgeon, he rasped nervously, "You were spying! That is most unseemly!"

"Look me in this eye!"

"I'm being serious."

"Don't be a jerk!"

Cedars and myrtles in the garden cast watery shadows on the drawing-room draperies, which stirred faintly in a spikenard-scented breeze. The Vicereine's Garden was a mournful geometry of fountains and myrtles, ponds and orderly paths. Between colonnades of cypresses, still black mirrors etched their formulas across the water. His Catholic Majesty's minister, a proud glint in his blue porcelain eyes, turned his back on that scoundrel Currito and retreated into the misty colonial pergola, jamming his monocle under an eyebrow. Green ivy had crept up the window overlooking the shadowy green garden. The Baron of Benicarlés pressed his forehead against the glass. Elephantine, brow wrinkled, most British, his face was a picture of despair. Curro and Merlin, from separate corners, gazed at him immersed in the fish-tank light of the folly's bay carved from scented woods evoking Oriental and eighteenth-century veneers and minuets danced by viceroys and almond-blossom princesses. Curro broke the spell, spitting cheekily through his fangs, "Isabelita, my darling, the way you ruffle your hair or push up your topknot, as far as yours truly goes, makes you as rank as a rajah! Isabelita, go hobnob with Tyrant."

"Bastard!"

"Isabelita, please, let's avoid a spanking!"

BOOK THREE
The Note

I

His Excellency the minister for Spain had ordered his carriage for half past six. Perfumed, powder-puffed, be-medaled, dressed with effeminate elegance, the Baron of Benicarlés placed his Panama, cane, and gloves on a console. Sucking in his stomach, he now laced his corset tight and retraced his steps to his boudoir. Carefully rolling up a trouser leg, so as not to crease it, he administered a shot of morphine. He stretched his leg, limped slightly, returned to the console, and put on his hat and gloves in front of the mirror. His bulging eyes quivered at the corner; his drooping mouth betrayed his roller-coastering thoughts. As he eased on his gloves, an image of Don Celes's yellow pair flashed though his mind. Now other snapshots hurtled through his memory, scampering as vigorously as young bulls in the ring. From acute angles and with ruptured grammar, words unleashed themselves with epigrammatic energy: futile jab of the goad; young steers from Guisando; hewn from granite. A lethal leap on the trampoline and a single thought hanging in the air, weightless and gaseous: Don Celes! What an entertaining ass! Splendid! The thought then dissolved into a vaguely playful feeling, transmuted into a succession of graphic, vivid intuitions suffused with the absurd logic of a dream. Don Celes was performing fantastic tricks with clownish sacks in a circus arena. It was that rotund whitey for real. Wow wee! Castelar had led him on to think that he would be appointed minister of the exchequer when he became prime minister.

The baron moved away from the console, walked through the drawing room and gallery, barked an order at his chambermaid, and went downstairs. The gleaming reflections from the stream flooded his mind. His carriage drew up, teetering on the edge of that quicksilver. The driver huffed and puffed as he reined in his horses. The lackey stood by the carriage door, frozen in a salute. These static, disconnected stills had a cruel and mocking impact under a cirrus sky, dominated by a green, crescent moon. Spain's minister rested his foot on the folding step and mentally spelled out his thoughts: "If they come up with a formula, I can't stand aside and make myself ridiculous for the sake of a quartet of grocers. It would be ridiculous to oppose the prohibition the diplomatic corps is calling for! Ridiculous!" His carriage rolled on. Mechanically, the baron raised a hand to his hat. Then thought, "Someone said hello. Who was it?" He squinted and registered the riotous street music and lights out of the corner of his eye. Spanish flags adorned bars and pawnshops. Again he squinted, recalling that drunken jamboree in the Spanish casino. Then he slid down through elusive shadows into a quiet corner of his consciousness, where he found himself enjoying a tedious atmosphere of refinement and isolation. Snippets of angular, broken grammar inscribed polyhedrons of thought in that blessed abyss, and acrobatic clauses swung back and forth on a trapeze of hidden connections. "Let them post me to Central Africa. Wherever there isn't a Spanish colony... Well, well, Don Celes! A grotesque fellow! What a brainwave that Castelar idea! I was quite cruel. I almost regret that. But the fellow had only come with his IOUs. It was right to nip him in the bud. An opportune ploy! And my debt can only increase... It's annoying. It's insulting. Diplomatic salaries are derisory. And the expenses!"

II

His carriage swung around a corner into the Portuguese Mothers Arcade. A cockfight was going on. Tense silence, broken by bursts of pandemonium. The baron lifted his monocle to look at the plebs, and then dropped it. A string of conflicting, vaguely literary reflections reminded him of life in the courts of Europe. A scent of orange blossom caressed him. His carriage trundled past the walls of a kitchen garden belonging to the nunnery. The sky was suffused with green light, like a sky painted by Veronese. The moon, as everywhere, wore a halo of Italian, English, and French verse. And lost in a subtle, pessimistic, nostalgic reverie the diplomatic roué let his confusion unravel in myriad triangles of connected thought. "Explanations! Why? Granite heads!" Via a chain of suggestions, threaded together by a quasi-cabalistic theory of images and words, he conjured up the illusion of a journey to exotic parts. He reviewed his collection of ivories. That totem with the naked paunch rippling with laughter looked like Don Celes. Once again his polyhedral *pensées* fleshed themselves out in words: "It will pain me to leave this country. I will take many memories with me. The loveliest friendships... It's been sweet and sour. Life, as everywhere... The men are worth infinitely more than the women. Just like Lisbon. There are real Apollos among the young. In all probability, I will never cease to miss these tropical climes. Ah the tremor of naked flesh!" His carriage rolled on. Jesus's Little Gate, the parade ground, Monotombo Square, the Portuguese Mothers Arcade, saddles, silver filigree, knives in a circle, gaming tables, strings of glass baubles that shimmer and shine.

III

Real Grand Guignol! Rowdies punching and stabbing opposite the English legation. The carriage slowed at the curb, the driver huffing and puffing as he reined in his horses. The lackey stood by the carriage door, frozen in salute. Alighting, the baron vaguely glimpsed a woman wearing a shawl. Her arms opened like black pincers. Was she summoning him? The vision vanished. Perhaps the old biddy was trying to get through to him. The baron lingered briefly on the step of his carriage and let his eyes take in the party in full swing on the Portuguese Mothers Arcade. He entered the legation. For a moment he thought he heard someone calling out to him; someone undoubtedly was. But he couldn't look around. He must deal with two ministers, two sticklers for protocol, raising their hats in tandem by way of welcome. They were standing on the bottom step of the staircase, under the chandelier's cascading light, opposite a mirror in which their reflected images appeared in a crazy oblique-angled jumble. The Baron of Benicarlés doffed his hat in turn, absentmindedly, mind miles away. The image of that old woman: her pincerlike arms beneath her shawl had distracted him. The echo of his own name, that voice that had perhaps called out to him, now also faded from his thoughts, as he remained lost in his recollections. He smiled mechanically at the two personages waiting for him beneath the resplendent chandelier. Exchanging polite nothings and pleasantries, he headed up the stairs sandwiched between the ministers for Chile and Brazil. Under his breath he hissed, "I think we musst be the firsst."

Vaguely worried that his trouser leg might still be rolled up, he glanced down at his feet. He could still feel the sting from the shot. A garter was working loose. What a disaster! And the minister for Brazil was sporting Don Celes's yellow gloves!

IV

Sir Jonnes H. Scott, His Gracious British Majesty's minister, dean of the diplomatic corps, expressed his puritanical scruples in limp French, punctuated by aspirated aitches. He was small and plumpish, with a jovial belly and a patriarch's baldpate. His face was a bright, ruddy-apple red and there was a dash of malign suspicion in his blue eyes that still sparkled with childish playfulness. "England has manifested in various ways its abhorrence at the way the most elementary laws of war are being flaunted. England is duty-bound to react when prisoners are being executed. Every pact and accord reached between civilized peoples is being violated."

The Latin American diplomats' mumbles of approval garnished the silence that broke out whenever the Honorable Sir Jonnes H. Scott sipped at his brandy and soda. Meanwhile Spain's minister was fluttering his eyelashes at Ecuador's minister, Dr. Aníbal Roncali, an electrically charged Creole, black curls, smoldering eyes, and handsome features, all blended together with subtle, somber charm, as in Chinese shadow theater. Germany's minister, Von Estrug, was quietly exchanging interminable Teutonic clauses with Count Chrispi, Austria's minister. France's representative kept his chin on his chest, doing his best to feign interest, his face half reflected in his monocle. The Honorable Sir Jonnes wiped his lips and continued: "A Christian sentiment of human solidarity offers us a chalice with which to commune in a joint action entreating respect for international legislation with regard to the lives and exchange of prisoners. Naturally, the government of the republic will not ignore the recommendations of the diplomatic corps. England's representative has a code of ethics, but at the same time he is interested in the opinions of the diplomatic corps. Ministers, this is why we have gathered here today. I apologize with due humility for the disturbance, but I did think it was my duty as dean to summon you."

The Latin American diplomats purred a perfunctory chorus of reverential yeses, congratulating His Gracious British Majesty's representative. Brazil's minister, rotund, jet-black, with the features of an Asiatic mandarin or bonze, spoke up, aligning his sentiments with those expressed by the Honorable Sir Jonnes H. Scott. He waved a pair of gloves that he'd twisted together. The Baron of Benicarlés was deeply irritated: those gyrating yellow gloves were getting in the way of his flirting. With a knowing smile, he got up and approached Ecuador's minister. "Those canary-colored mittens our Brazilian colleague is showing off are something loathsome!"

The first secretary and acting minister for the French legation explained: "Cream actually. The latest mode from the court of St. James."

The Baron of Benicarlés envisioned Don Celes with ironic glee. Ecuador's minister now climbed to his feet, ebony curls in a frenzy, and began to declaim. The Baron of Benicarlés, a great stickler for protocol, smiled a long-suffering smile at his posturing and torrential metaphors. Dr. Aníbal Roncali suggested that the diplomats from Spanish America should hold an initial meeting, to be presided over by the Spanish minister. Bracing their wings before taking heroic flight, the eaglets snuggled up to Mamma Eagle. The Latin American diplomats muttered agreement. The Baron of Benicarlés bowed: he acknowledged the honor on behalf of the mother country. Tilting his head to one side and smiling like a syrupy nun, eyes beady and sly, he clasped the Ecuadorian's ebony hands between his odalisque fingers and spoke fastidiously: "My dear colleague, I accept with but one stipulation, that you sit next to me and serve as secretary!"

Dr. Aníbal Roncali felt a desperate desire to liberate his hand from the Spanish minister's insistent grasp. A puerile, timorous angst repelled him. He recalled a painted hag who'd caught his eye when he went to the lycée. A horrible hag, as insistent as a rule of grammar! But the roué went on clasping his hand and seemed on the verge of sinking it into his bosom. He spoke with ponderous emphasis, beamed ecstatically, and conducted himself with appalling cynicism. Ecuador's minister made an effort to escape. "Just a minute, Minister, I must say hello to Sir Scott."

The Baron of Benicarlés stiffened and inserted his monocle. "And am I not owed the same pleasure, dear colleague?"

Dr. Aníbal Roncali nodded, ruffling his curls, and slunk off, his back almost tingling, as if he could still hear that painted hag hissing at him on his way to the lycée. He edged himself into the circle that was busy slapping perfidious Albion's evangelical plenipotentiary on the back. The baron stood up, felt his corset slither down around his hips, and walked over to the U.S. ambassador. Meanwhile the excessive rapture of the huddle sending up incense to British diplomacy attracted the formidable Von Estrug, representative of the German Empire. Saffron-tinted Count Chrispi, the representative of the Austro-Hungarian Empire, was a mere satellite in his orbit. The Yankee spoke in a confidential tone: "The Honorable Sir

Jonnes Scott has eloquently expressed the humanitarian sentiments animating the diplomatic corps. There can be no doubt about that. But do those sentiments justify intervention in the republic's internal affairs, even if only at the level of offering advice? Doubtless the republic is undergoing a profound revolutionary upheaval. Repression is necessary and must be adequate to the task. We witness executions, cover our ears, close our eyes, speak of advice... Gentlemen, we are too susceptible. General Banderas's government is acting responsibly and knows what it is doing. In the government's view such rigor is necessary. Is the diplomatic corps really in a position to advise?"

The German minister, a blue-blooded Jew who'd made a fortune in Bolivian rubber, manifested blunt approval in Spanish, English, and German. Severe, bald Count Chrispi also agreed, twirling his saffron mustache in the purest French. His Spanish Majesty's representative was undecided. The three diplomats—the Yankee, the Teuton, and the Austrian, rehearsing a coordinated threefold dissent—had alerted him to their conspiratorial path. He felt genuine sorrow, for he knew that in the diplomatic world, his world, all the cabals operated without appeal to the minister for Spain. The Honorable Sir Jonnes H. Scott had pronounced yet again, "May I request that my respected colleagues be seated."

The huddles separated. The ministers took their seats, bowing and whispering to one another, humming like the Tower of Babel. Trawling his Puritan conscience for righteous words, Sir Scott again offered the honorable diplomatic corps that chalice overflowing with humanitarian sentiments. After labyrinthine debate it was agreed to issue a "Note" to be signed by twenty-seven nations. An act with impact! Cabled laconically in true telegraphese, news of the Note soon sped its away around the world through the portals of the world's greatest newspapers: "Santa Fe de Tierra Firme. The honorable diplomatic corps has presented a Note to the government of the republic. The Note, to which the diplomatic corps attaches great importance, advises the immediate closure of all liquor stores and demands that the protection of foreign legations and banks be reinforced."

PART SEVEN

The Green Grimace

BOOK ONE

Tyrant at Play

I

GENERALITO Banderas slotted the metal quoit in the frog's mouth. Spectacular in rings and necklaces, sitting between the grindstone and the coffeepot, Doña Lupita umpired the game from beneath a striped parasol, encircled by her brightly colored flounces. "Frog!"

II

"Croak! Croak!"

Smarmy and barmy, Nachito looked on from the friends' enclosure—another of Tyrant's terrible tasteless jokes. His green grimace churned up the poisonous scorn that still circulated through the crevices of his mind until he launched into an outburst of hypochondriac sarcasm: "Master Veguillas, you're my partner in the next round. Try to live up to your reputation. Don't fuck up. You're shaking like a reed in the breeze! How pale you are, my fine fellow! You need a glass of lemonade. Master V, if you don't calm down, you'll ruin your record. And don't curl your lip at me, Master V! Lemon cordial is just what the doctor orders for souls in crisis. Have a word with that old camp follower and drink a toast with our guests. Bid a cheerful farewell and we'll all pray for you when you kick the bucket!"

Nacho groaned and staggered and turned white, his ugly visage swollen by tears. "That street nymph was the death of me!"

"Don't speak in riddles!"

"Generalito, the Holy Souls' little japes were what did me in! I appeal against my martyrdom! Hope! Give me hope! The rosebush of hope flowers in the most barren of sand dunes! Man cannot live without hope. A bird is full of hope and sings though the branch beneath him breaks, because he knows he has wings. The light of dawn brings hope. My Generalito, all beings wear the green mantle of the Deity! Her voice sings within every soul! The light from her eyes reaches into the darkest dungeon! Consoles the man on death row! Holds out a promise of a reprieve from the Supreme Court!"

Kid Santos extracted the schoolmasterish handkerchief from his frock coat and wiped his skull. "Chop-chop! Such eloquence, Master V! Dr. Sánchez Ocaña must have taught you well in Santa Mónica! Chop-chop!"

Tyrant's entourage chuckled at his barbed dig.

III

Bowing and scraping, Doña Lupita dispensed a rainbow of refreshment on a sunbeam. Kid Santos alternately sipped lemonade and peered at the old hag: clusters of coral, an insinuating groveling Oriental nuts-and-honey smile. "Chop-chop! Doña Lupita, I'm inclined to believe you've got Queen Cleopatra's nose. A dustup over a few smashed glasses and you've succeeded in wreaking havoc in the republic. You're more scheming than the honorable diplomatic corps. How many of your glasses did Colonel de la Gándara break? Doña Lupita, for less than a boliviano you drove him into the arms of the revolution. The nose of the pharaoh queen couldn't have done better. Doña Lupita, the debt owed to justice that you've involved me in has unraveled a fatal skein of events. It's the inspiration for Colonel de la Gándara's rebellion. It has landed Doña Rosa Pintado's lad inside Santa Mónica. Baby Roach, la Taracena, is appealing against the closing of her flophouse, and we now have a Note from His Catholic Majesty's minister to answer. Our bonds with the mother country may be broken. And here you are, my dear, entirely unmoved by all these catastrophes! To cap it off, four broken glasses from your side table, a paperweight, a miserable bagatelle—thanks to this I may have to deprive myself of the pleasure of Master V's froggy songs."

"Croak! Croak!"

Trying to work his way back into Tyrant's good graces, Nacho V responded to his scorn by honking and hopping like a frog.

With sour Quakerish sarcasm Tyrant berated him: "Don't play the buffoon, Master V. These good friends who are about to sentence you won't be swayed by your batrachian tomfoolery. They are cultured minds who, to say the very least, have seen the parliaments of old Europe in full swing."

"Juvenal and Jonathan Swift!"

Distinguished whitey stroked his ginger whiskers, his rotund belly and his cheeks grown flabby from uttering flattering words. The old camp follower crossed herself. "I swear by the Holy Virgin, it's Old Nick that done it!"

"And slotted in one!"

"If the world was that messed up the holy saints would go straight to Hell!"

"A cracking declaration, Doña Lupita. But isn't your soul even a little bit troubled by having unleashed so much turmoil, so many bolts from the blue?"

"Boss, don't strike fear into my soul!"

"Doña Lupita, you shudder, don't you, at the thought of your responsibilities before eternity?"

"I am praying for all I'm worth!"

IV

Tyrant Banderas looked out at the trail. "Chop-chop! Will whoever has the sharpest eyes please let me know whose troops those are that are heading this way. Isn't the resplendent rider at the head of the pack the renowned Don Roque Cepeda?"

Escorted by four Indian riders, Don Roque stopped at the other side of the fence by the gate. In the light of the setting sun, the horseman's bronzed temples, golden sombrero, and silvery, sweating colt gave him the aura of a Romanesque saint. Tyrant Banderas adopted Quakerishly measured tones as he embarked on an absurd welcome: "So pleased to see you in this neck of the woods! It was Santos Banderas's duty to consult with you with regard to a few pressing questions, of course, but my dear Don Roque, why have you put yourself to so much trouble? It was I, yours truly, who was under the obligation to visit you in your abode in order to offer my apologies and those of my entire government. Which is why I dispatched one of my aides to request an audience with you, and here you are, and it is so very kind of you to take this trouble when I, Santos Banderas, should really have been the one to have taken the initiative."

Don Roque dismounted and Tyrant hugged him warmly. They had a long, confidential exchange on the friars' lookout bench, opposite the becalmed equatorial sea where the sun blazed a path as it flamed down through the western sky. "Chop-chop! So pleased to see you."

"Mr. President, sir, I didn't want to join the campaign without first speaking to you. It is a question of courtesy and of my attachment to the republic. Mr. President, sir, your aide, my former colleague, Lauro Méndez, secretary for Foreign Affairs, came to visit me. Our conversation spurred me to take action, and I expect you, Mr. President, sir, are aware of the outcome."

"The honorable secretary acted incorrectly if he failed to inform you that he was acting under my instructions. Transparency is the name of my game. Don Roque, my friend, our independence as a nation is in danger, under siege from ambitious foreign powers. The honorable diplomatic corps—a thieves' den of colonial interests—is shooting us in the back with the slanderous Note it is cabling everywhere. Malign agencies are being deployed by these foreign diplomats to defame the Republic of Santa Fe. The Yankees and Europeans are equally greedy for our rubber, mines, and oil. True patriots must look ahead to a time of deepest anguish. We may even face military intervention, and that's why I wanted this audience with you. I want to propose a truce. Chop-chop!"

"A truce?"

"A truce until the international issues are resolved. You can set the conditions. I will begin by offering an amnesty to all political prisoners who didn't take up arms."

Don Roque muttered, "Amnesty is the correct policy and one that I fully support. Many, however, were unjustly accused of conspiracy."

"Everybody will be amnestied."

"And will the election really be free? What about the secret police? Will they refrain from harassing the opposition parties and the voters?"

"The election will be free and the law will be observed. What more can I say? I want peace for the country. I am offering you peace. Santos Banderas is not the vulgar power-hungry monster that dissidents like to caricature. I only want what is best for the republic. The happiest day in my life will be the day I, like Cincinnatus, can return to my farm in the outback. In a word, you and your friends will recover your freedom and the full exercise of your civil rights. As a loyal patriot, however, you must strive to return the revolution to the paths of legality. But if the people cast their ballots for you, I will be the first to respect their sovereign will. I admire your humanitarian ideals, Don Roque. I feel bitter that I am unable to share your optimism. Therein lies my tragedy as a ruler! You, a Creole from one of the best Creole families, dismiss Creole interests. While I, a plain Indian, lack any faith in the virtues and abilities of my race. You stand before me like a man who has seen the light; your touching faith in the destiny of indigenous peoples reminds me of Bartolomé de las Casas. You wish to scatter the shades that three hundred years of colonial rule has cast around the Indian soul. How admirable! There is nothing Santos Banderas would like more. Don Roque, after present circumstances have been successfully dealt with, defeat me, annihilate me, demonstrate the slumbering potential of my race through a victory that I will be the first to celebrate. Your victory will be a permanent victory for the Indians. From that day forth, they will hold sway over the destiny of our nation. Don Roque, go propagandize as freely as you like, work your miracle within the law, and, believe me, I will be the first to celebrate. Don Roque, I thank you for listening. Now will you please state any objections, as frankly as you wish. I don't want you to give me your word now and then find you are unable to keep to it. Consult the leading lights among your allies. Offer them an olive branch from Santos Banderas."

Don Roque gave him a look of such serenely ingenuous sincerity that it was impossible to miss his qualms. "A truce!"

"A truce. A hallowed union. Don Roque, let us defend the independence of the fatherland."

Tyrant Banderas waved his arms pathetically. He could hear his cronies in the twilit garden mocking and teasing Master Veguillas.

V

Don Roque cantered off into the distance waving his handkerchief. From behind the gate, Kid Santos waved his top hat in return. Horse and rider were soon hidden in fields of tall maize, though the arm and handkerchief continued to wave, "Chop-chop! A pigeon!"

The mummy went on joking and grimacing and drooling poison. He looked at the old camp follower who, seated between the coffeepot and the grindstone and encircled by her flounces, was telling her rosary beads, horrified at the prospect of a night of holy terror. She stood up at a sign from Tyrant. "Generalito, the world's tangled ways may lead the holiest of men to the cauldrons of Hell."

"My dear, you *really* should amputate that Cleopatra's nose of yours."

"If that would *really* sort out this world, I'd go snub-nosed tonight."

"A skirmish over four glasses on your table opened a door for Lucifer to step in. Consider our now disgraced melodious friend, charged with treachery! He'll probably be sentenced to death!"

"And was the smashing of my glassware really to blame?"

"Future historians will have to figure that one out. Master Veguillas, bid goodbye to this old camp follower. Forgive her. Show your generosity of spirit. Put your cloak on, and astonish these jokers with your magnanimity."

"Juvenal and Jonathan Swift!"

The mummy grinned sourly in whitey's direction. "Illustrious Don Celestino, it's up to you to get me some mileage out of this. Neither Juvenal nor Jonathan Swift: Santos Banderas. The wonder of these southern shores. Chop-chop!"

BOOK TWO

The Terrace at the Club

I

Dr. Carlos Esparza, the minister for Uruguay, assumed a worldly air as, tongue-in-cheek, he listened to the confidences of his close colleague, Dr. Aníbal Roncali, the minister for Ecuador. They were dining at the Rifle Club. "The Baron of Benicarlés has created a very trying situation. You know the brilliant track record I have established as a seducer of women, and that I've got no reason to be afraid of gossip. However, the minister for Spain continues to behave in a most inappropriate fashion. The way he titters! The glances he gives me!"

"Sure, buddy. That's called passion."

Bald, shortsighted, and refined, Dr. Esparza jammed his tortoiseshell monocle into an eye socket. Dr. Aníbal Roncali stared, unsure whether to grin or look mortified. "You're kidding."

The minister for Uruguay apologized with a sarcastic sweep of the hand.

"Aníbal, it looks like you're hand in glove with the Baron of Benicarlés. That could spark a diplomatic row, not to mention complaints from the mother country!"

The minister for Ecuador gestured impatiently, fluttering his curls. "You continue to jest."

"What do you intend to do?"

"I haven't the slightest."

"I assume you're not about to accept the post of secretary to the grand project you were so eloquently describing the other night?"

"No doubt."

"All because of your jackassing it around . . . !"

"Spare me wordplay, please."

"No pun intended. Yes, I'm sure it would be a great opportunity for you, and you just can't think of any reasons to refuse. The eagle and its eaglets opening their wings to take heroic flight. What a blithe spirit you! What a lover of the lyre!"

"Dear Doctor, will you please stop kidding around."

"Lyrical, sentimental, sensitive, sensible!" proclaimed Rubén Darío, the swan from Nicaragua. "And that's why you'll never drive a wedge between the minister for Spain's diplomatic initiatives and his flirting."

"Let's be serious, Doctor. What is your opinion of Sir Jonnes's suggestion?"

"It's a first step."

"And what do you perceive will be the effect of the Note?"

"Qui lo sá! The Note may open the way for other Notes . . . It depends on the president's response. Sir Jonnes is so very affable and evangelical that all he requests is that the West Company Limited be compensated at the cost of twenty million. As so often, a viper lurks among the sweet-smelling violets of humanitarian sentiment."

"No doubt the Note is a way of testing the waters. But how will the general react? Will the government agree to the compensation?"

"Unfortunately, this America of ours continues to be a colony of Europe . . . On this occasion, however, the government of Santa Fe is not going to allow its arm to be twisted. The government is quite aware that the ideals of the revolution are in direct conflict with the monopolies these companies enjoy. Tyrant Banderas is not going to die from a diplomatic goring. Selfish Creoles, landowners, and foreign investors are coming together to prop him up. In the end, the government could refuse compensation, confident that the great powers are not going to support radical revolutionaries. The emancipation of the Indian is of course inevitable. It would be unwise to shut one's eyes to that. But something may be inevitable and still not be imminent. Death is inevitable, but our lives are devoted to keeping it at bay. The diplomatic corps acts reasonably when it defends the existence of these old and, yes, now declining political entities. We're the crutches of geezers who mean to hang on for eternity like those philosophers of old."

The breeze rippled the draperies and the blue curtain of the marina, illuminated by the opalescent lanterns on masts, glistened in the deep distant darkness.

II

The minister for Ecuador and the minister for Uruguay walked onto the terrace in a billowing cloud of cigar smoke. When he saw them, Tu-Lag-Thi, the Japanese minister, sat up in his bamboo rocking chair and greeted them with the feigned affability of Oriental diplomats. He was savoring his frothy coffee and his gold-rimmed glasses lay open on an English newspaper. The Latin American ministers went over to him. Bows, smiles, the whole solemn charade of nods and handshakes and French chitchat. The servant, a vacuous mulatto forever attentive to every diplomatic demand, dragged over two rocking chairs. Dr. Roncali set his curls a-dancing and launched into gushing oratory, singing the praises of the beauty of the night, the moon, and the sea. Tu-Lag-Thi, the Japanese minister, listened, scowling darkly, his face drawn. His lips framed his gleaming dentures like purple welts. His slant eyes shone with malign suspicion. An admirer of everything exotic and novel, Dr. Esparza commented, "Nighttime in Japan must be wonderful!"

"Oh! Undoubtedly! And tonight is not without a certain Japanese cachet!"

Tu-Lag-Thi's voice sounded as flat as an out-of-tune piano and his movements were as stiff as a windup doll with rusty springs, an unholy inner life of coiled wire. He grimaced a dark, affected smile:

"My dear colleagues, earlier on I was unable to solicit your opinions. How important do you believe the Note to be?"

"It's a first step!"

Dr. Esparza qualified his words with an ambiguous smile. The Japanese minister continued: "One understood it as such, naturally. Will the diplomatic corps remain in accord? Where is this all going? The English minister is driven by humanitarian imperatives, but his generosity may be checked. None of the foreign colonies has any sympathy with revolutionary ideas. The Spanish colony, so numerous, so influential, and in every way so tightly linked to the Creole class, is frankly hostile to the agrarian reforms of the Zamalpoa Plan. At this very moment—according to my inside information—the Spanish colony is preparing to affirm its allegiance to the government of the republic. Perhaps in the end Honorable Sir Scott will find himself the lone supporter of his humanitarian campaign."

Dr. Carlos Esparza's myopic eyes twinkled maliciously. "My dear colleague, it's all too obvious diplomacy is not born of the Gospels."

Tu-Lag-Thi mewled mournfully in response: "Japan believes that the Rights of Man take priority over the interests of any of its citizens resident here. But in our mutual exchange of confidences, or rather indiscretions, I cannot hide that I view the moral support some of our colleagues have offered to the laudable sentiments of the English minister with great pessimism. Nor as a man of honor can I credit the insinuations and slanders published by the dailies that are in tight with the government of the republic. The West Company! How abominable!"

Tu-Lag-Thi's final truculent blast wound down to a lisping hiss as he flashed an obsequious Asiatic grin. Dr. Aníbal Roncali stroked his mustache while his quavering lips came up with an emotion-laden paragraph. He spoke with tremendous nervous energy, working his black curls into a frenzy, until they stood up straight like lizards' tails: "Dr. Banderas cannot order the liquor shops to shut their doors. If he does, there will be riots. These fiestas are bacchanalia for half-breeds and bums!"

III

Echoes from the fair floated in on the breeze. Strings of toy lanterns danced along the street. At the far end a merry-go-round went round and round, lights blinking, creating a strident, hysterical clatter that hypnotized the cats crouched on the eaves. The wind hummed and performed acrobatic feats with the toy lanterns that swung back and forth in time, and the street winked. In the distance, the shadowy fortress of Saint-Martin of the Mostenses loomed up through the luminous haze.

BOOK THREE
A Time for Buffoons

I

TYRANT Banderas, at the window, pointed his telescope at the city of Santa Fe. "What delightful illuminations! They're *so* pretty, aren't they!"

Cronies and hangers-on gathered around the steps to the stars. The green grimace perched at the top. "The people cannot be denied their bread and circuses. The illuminations are *so* pretty!"

Muffled shots reached them on a sea breeze from Santa Mónica. "Liberated from pernicious propaganda, the people mean well! And discipline does them good!"

The circle of buddies expanded. Tyrant's utterances held them rooted to the spot.

II

Tyrant Banderas descended from his pinnacle, entered the circle of aides and hangers-on, and extracted Master Veguillas with a tweak of the ear. "We would like to hear your froggy concert one last time. How's your throat? Need to gargle?"

The band of toadies lapped up this broadside and laughed grotesquely. Nachito was stunned. "How can you expect a corpse to be tuneful?"

"How very wrong of you not to placate your judges with a ditty!

Sirs, this good old friend appears before you accused of treason. Had his trickery gone undiscovered, he might have sunk the lot of you. You will recall how last night, speaking in confidence, I informed you that I intended to bring Colonel Domiciano de la Gándara to justice in light of his subversive activities. And these words, meant only for the ears of Santos Banderas's closest friends, these words were divulged. Advise me now what the proper punishment should be for this divulger of secrets. The witnesses for the defense have been summoned and, should you agree, will now make their statements. Master V himself has stated that a sleepwalking courtesan, having been hypnotized by one Dr. Polish, succeeded in divining his thoughts. We appear to be embroiled in an episode from a novel by Alexandre Dumas! This literally entrancing doctor who endows flophouse strumpets with prophetic powers must be a descendant of Joseph Bálsamo who has fallen on hard times. Do you remember the novel? A fascinating feuilleton! And we are living it out in the flesh! Take a look: our Master Veguillas rivals the genius of the mulatto Dumas! Now he will tell us where it was he and the rebel Domiciano de la Gándara intended to escape to."

Nachito whimpered. "All we did was chat on the way out of the establishment."

"You were both plastered?"

"Boss, it was the fiesta! The whole of Santa Fe was drunk! That joker suddenly panicked while we were chatting and rushed across the street into a house. Some poor soul happened to open the door. I reacted like an idiot, flapping my ears like a frightened llama.

"Could you describe the establishment where you had gone to carouse?"

"Generalito, don't make me blush. It's far too profane a spot to mention here in this audience chamber. I'm red with embarrassment in the presence of your noble patrician self."

"Answer the question. What dive was it that you went to with Colonel de la Gándara, and what did you confide to him in said place? Master V, you knew an arrest warrant had been issued. Drunkenly, you let some word escape that alerted him—and allowed him to escape."

"Do all my years of loyalty count for nothing?"

"The act may have been unpremeditated, but a state of inebriation is not an extenuating circumstance in the courthouse of Santos Banderas. You are a piss-pot and you spend your nights bingeing in bordellos. Santos Banderas knows your every move. I'm warning you that truth and truth alone will cool my ire. Master V, I would like to give you a hand and drag you from the quagmire where you're floundering helplessly. You know treason incurs a very harsh sentence under our laws."

"Mr. President, sir, there are circumstances in life that cause total panic, circumstances that could come straight out of a novel. On the night in question I visited a psychic pussycat."

"A psychic pussycat that inhabits a cathouse where you court her?"

"Well, that's what happened last night down at Baby Roach's joint. I want to make a full statement and clear my conscience. We were both in a state of sin. It was the Day of the Dead last night, Generalito! Gentlemen, I swear on my word of honor that that dark-skinned girl lit a holy candle that revealed all these mysteries. She could read minds!"

"Drunken fantasies, Master V. You were blotto when you took up with the hooker. In vile commerce with a common whore you betrayed me, you disclosed my secrets. Well the first thing you need, in order to cool your burning flesh, is some time in the stocks. Master V, go into that corner, kneel, and lift your thoughts—try!—to the Supreme Being. This crew of select colleagues will then pass sentence on you, and a sentence of death is not at all out of the question. But Master V, the eyewitnesses you have described will speak in your defense, and if their statements exonerate you, I, for one, will be delighted. Colonel López de Salamanca, sir, I request that immediately and by any means necessary you produce the doctor and the whore!"

III

The Honorable Colonel López de Salamanca, who'd been4 loitering by the doorpost, thrust Dr. Polish into the room. Lupita *la Romántica* was peering over his shoulder. Tall and bewhiskered, with a broad domed forehead and the locks of a sage, Dr. Polish sported a dinner jacket with two sashes over his chest and a rosette in the lapel. He greeted them with a pompously sweeping bow and tucked his top hat under his arm. "Allow me to render homage to the Supreme Highness of the republic. Michaelis Lugín, Ph.D., University of Cairo and initiate in the secret knowledge of the Brahmins of Bengal."

"Do you subscribe to the teachings of Allan Kardec?"

"No, I am a modest disciple of Mesmer. Kardecian spiritualism is a childish travesty of ancient necromancy—the art of summoning the dead that derives from Egyptian papyrus and Chaldean masonry. The word designating these phenomena derives from two Greek ones."

"This doctor of ours expresses himself very doctorally! And does your renown as the prophet from Cairo allow you to earn your bread?"

"President, sir, my merit, such as it is, is not manifested through money or wealth. *My* mission is to propagate the doctrines of theosophy and to prepare people for the next era of miracles. The shadow of New Christ walks the paths of the planet."

"Do you admit to employing magnetism in order to put this girl into a trance?"

"I admit to conducting the occasional experiment. It is a remarkable field."

"List each and every experiment you have conducted."

"President, sir, if you so wish, you can see the programs of experiments I have conducted in the coliseums and academies of St. Petersburg, Vienna, Naples, Berlin, Paris, London, Lisbon, and Rio de Janeiro. Recently prestigious publications in Chicago and Philadelphia have been devoted to debating my theories on karma and bio-magnetic suggestion. The Havana Club of the Theosophical Star has conferred the title of Perfect Brother on me. The empress of Austria does me the honor of regularly consulting me about the meaning of her dreams. I possess secrets that I shall never reveal. The president of the French Republic and the king of Prussia tried to bribe me when I performed in their capital cities. To no avail! The path of theosophy teaches one to scorn titles and wealth. If I have your permission, I will place my photograph albums and press cuttings at the disposition of the president."

"And how come somebody so versed in such austere doctrines and so highly initiated into theosophy happens to be bingeing in a bordello? Would you be so good as to scientifically illuminate and justify such apparently aberrant behavior?"

"Mr. President, sir, allow me to call upon my medium. Señorita, overcome your natural modesty and tell these gentlemen whether concupiscence mediated at all. President, sir, a scientific interest in bio-magnetic experiments, without ulterior motives, regulates my activities. I visited the bordello because people had told me about this young lady. I wanted to meet her and, if at all possible, lift her life to another, more perfect circle. Señorita, did I not offer you redemption?"

"Pay my debts, you mean? No, it was Master V who rattled on about that all night."

"Señorita Guadalupe, do you not remember how with fatherly concern I proposed that you come with me on my pilgrim's path?"

"Go on stage, you mean!"

"And demonstrate to incredulous audiences the occult, demiurgic powers that slumber within our human clay. You rejected my proposal, and I was forced to withdraw and lament my failures. President, sir, I think by now I must have allayed any suspicion regarding the purity of my actions. In Europe the most renowned men of science are engaged in research on these phenomena. Mesmerism is widely studied in German universities."

"You will now repeat, step by step, the experiments you engaged in last night with that girl."

"President, sir, I am completely at your disposal. Yes, I can offer you a select program of similar experiments."

"As is due to her sex, the girl will be the first to be questioned. Master Veguillas has claimed that at some stage a magnetic flow from the aforesaid allowed her to read his thoughts."

The girl glanced at the paste jewels on her fingers and said, "If I had powers like that, I wouldn't be up to my neck in debt to Baby Roach. Master V, you know that."

"Lupita, you bio-magnetic viper."

"What are you talking about? After I gave you all that ammoniac!"

"Lupita, confess you were in a trance last night. You read my thoughts while that fool Domiciano was making the rounds on the dance floor. Then you tipped him off with a glance."

"Master V, both of you were plastered! I just wanted you out of my room."

"Lupita, you guessed what I was thinking. Lupita, you know how to commerce with the Spirits. Don't deny that Dr. Polish put you to sleep and you served him as a medium."

"Yes, indeed, this young lady is a most remarkable case of magnetic lucidity. So that our distinguished audience can better appreciate these phenomena, she will now take a seat in the limelight. Señorita Medium, if you will allow me."

He took her hand and ceremonially led her to the center of the room. The girl tiptoed, eyes down, innocent as can be, the keyboard of her nails hovering above Dr. Polish's white gloves.

"Chop-chop!"

IV

The Indian mummy's sarcastic grimace was evergreen from old age. Dr. Polish plucked his magic wand, forged from seven metals, out of his dinner jacket and touched Lupita's eyelids. He concluded with the most courteous of bows and a wave of his wand. The strumpet sighed and swooned. Kneeling in his corner, Veguillas waited on the miracle: the light of his innocence was about to shine. The Lupita show bewitched him there and then with the hallowed magic of serial fiction: he hoped in his heart of hearts that those mysteries would return him to Tyrant's grace and favor. He shuddered. The green grimace champed on the rusty silence. "Chop-chop! You will now repeat, step by step, as I believe I already requested, the experiments you performed on this young lady last night."

"President, sir, telepathy can assume three temporal forms: past, present, and future. This triple phenomenon is rarely present in a single medium. It is usually dispersed. Señorita Guadalupe's telepathic powers do not extend beyond the circle of the present. Past and future are sealed to her. Telepathically speaking, the nearest yesterday is the remotest past for her. This young lady is absolutely unequipped to repeat a previous experiment. Absolutely! This young lady is somewhat underdeveloped as a medium. An uncut diamond! I await the president's orders so I may offer him a select program of similar experiments, insofar as it is within my powers."

A sour grimace wrinkled Tyrant's face. "Doctor, don't seek to dodge your obligations to me. It is my wish that she repeat every one of last night's experiments in the cathouse."

"President, sir, I can only perform similar experiments. The medium cannot look back into time. In that sense, she really is quite limited as a clairvoyant. She can read thoughts, witness an event at a distance, or even guess a number the president might care to think of."

"A bitch as clever as all that, and she's a pro in a whorehouse?"

"The great neurosis of hysteria as described within modern science could afford a most likely explanation. Señorita, the president will deign to think of a number. You will take his hand and say the number out loud so we can all hear it. Loud and very clear, Señorita Medium."

"Seven!"

"Seven as in seven daggers! Chop-chop!"

Nachito moaned from exile. "That was the spell you used to read my thoughts yesterday!"

Tyrant Banderas swiveled around, ever the sarcastic sourpuss. "Why do you visit evil dives, *mon vieux*?"

"Boss, even the Psalms say man is frail."

Tyrant resumed his saturnine pose and stared suspiciously at the hussy. She was swooning in her chair, hairpins loose and topknot slithering like a black cobra.

Tyrant Banderas stepped into the circle of cronies. "As kids we were all treated to similar miracles for a few pennies: so many diplomas and sashes and so little to show for them. I'm beginning to see just what a phony you are, and I'm going to have those flowing Germanic locks chopped off. You have no right to them."

"President, sir, I am a foreigner and an exile who has taken shelter under the flag of this noble republic. I teach the truth to the people, steering them away from materialist positivism. My little experiments give the proletariat a tangible notion of the supernatural world. The people are ennobled when they can look down into the abyss of mystery!"

"Don Cruz! As he's got such a silver tongue, only shave half his head."

Tyrant's grimace rippled biliously. His tame sweeney's black bunched fingers handed him a hairy hodgepodge. "It's a wig, boss!"

V

The whore sighed as she came around, reemerging with a spasm on the frontiers of this world while the Indian mummy, from the pinnacle of his steps, aimed his telescope at the city. The wildly winking illuminations harbored a tumult of explosions, fire and bells and urgent blasts from military bugles. "Chop-chop! We've got action! Don Cruz, lay out my military apparel."

The watchman in the tower had unclipped his bayonet from the moon and was shooting at the shadows full of alarums. The cathedral bells chimed midnight, and Tyrant issued orders from the top of his steps: "Major del Valle, take some men with you and go see if the garrison began the shoot-out."

At the door, Major del Valle ran into the grinning valet bearing the general's uniform and saber, and the saber clattered noisily to the floor. Tyrant bellowed and stamped, beside himself with rage. The steps shook and the telescope tottered. "Idiots, don't touch it! What an omen! How do you read that, Dr. Magic?"

In a flash of inspiration, the mountebank took in the room, the fear spreading on every face, and Tyrant's rampant superstition. He responded, "Under these circumstances, my oracle is dumb."

"And couldn't this honest young girl, who on other occasions has displayed clear vision, tell us what's going in Santa Fe? Doctor, sir, please put Señorita Medium to sleep and interrogate her. I'm off to put on my uniform. And nobody touch my saber!"

A loud clash of weapons echoed down the moonlit cloisters. Troops arrived to reinforce the palace guard. The dark-skinned girl sighed in response to the bald mountebank's magnetic powers. Her eyes rolled up to contemplate the mystery. "Señorita Medium, what do you see?"

VI

The cathedral clock falls silent. The twelve chimes still echo in the air, terrifying the combs of the weathercocks. Cats on the roofs query one another and bodies in nightgowns peer down from attics. The Portuguese Mothers bell clangs crazily. A string of bulls and oxen butt around the arcade in full flight, cowbells tinkling. Gunpowder blasts. Military bugles blast. A gaggle of bald, nightshirted nuns rushes at the profaned convent door, screaming devoutly. In remote reaches, crossfire crackles. Restless horses, turmoil, panic, fear. Conflicting tides of humanity. Escaped, bright-eyed tigers lick the cornerstones of houses. Two fleeting shadows drag a black piano across a moonlit terrace. Behind them, smoke billows out of the open trapdoor between tongues of fire. The two shadows, clothes alight, run, holding hands, across the parapet of the terrace and hurl themselves into the street, still holding hands. And the moon, wearing a patch of dark cloud, plays blindman's buff with the stars above the revolutionized Santa Fe de Tierra Firme.

VII

Lupita *la Romántica* sighs in a magnetic trance, the whites of her eyes fixed on mystery.

EPILOGUE

I

"Chop-chop!"

Tyrant keeps a wary, suspicious eye on the defenses, orders sandbanks and parapets be built, visits bulwarks and trenches, issuing orders: "Chop-chop!"

Enraged by his fainthearted warriors, he swears that cowards and traitors will be harshly punished. How galling to fail in his first goal: to descend on the revolutionized city and teach it an exemplary, bloody lesson. Surrounded by his aides, taciturn and contemptuous, he withdraws from the front after haranguing his squads of veterans, the advance units on the Field of the Frog: "Chop-chop."

II

Before dawn he realized that he was under siege from revolutionary partisans and insurgent battalions from the Santa Fe garrison. He climbed the belfry without bells and studied the positions and tactics of his attackers. The enemy was scattered along twilight paths and looked to be in good military shape. The besiegers were still reinforcing the approaches with trenches and parallels. Informed of the danger, Tyrant Banderas grimaced more greenly yet. Two devious women were digging with their hands around the Indian buried up to his waist in the monastery's fallow ground. "Those old bitches have already given me up for lost! What are you doing, idiot sentinel?"

The sentinel slowly took aim. "It's difficult to get a clear target!"

"Put a bullet in the bastard and in them, too, for good measure!"

The sentinel fired, and his shots could be heard up and down the front line. The two women fell in a heap on either side of the Indian, amid the gun smoke, in the terrifying silence that then descended. And the Indian, with a hole in his head, waved his arms in a farewell to the stars. Generalito: "Chop-chop!"

III

At the first onslaught the soldiers in one frontline unit deserted. Tyrant saw it all from his tower. "Bugger! I knew you'd run for it in my time of need! Don Cruz, you'll make a prophet yet!"

He made that remark because his renowned sweeney often whispered tales of betrayal in his ear. Meanwhile, the two sides continued to exchange fire. The insurgents were seeking to tighten their grip on the besieged fortress, cutting off any hope of escape. They lined up cannons, but, before they opened fire, Colonel de la Gándara rode out in front of the lines on a handsome steed. He risked his life by crossing the battlefield and shouted an invitation to surrender. Tyrant in his tower: "Bastard buccaneer, I should have shot you in the back!"

He stuck his head out over the soldiers lined up at the foot of the tower and ordered them to fire. They obeyed but shot so high that it was clear they weren't shooting to kill. "You're shooting at the skies, you sons of bitches!"

At that very moment, riding out on a foray that was much too sweeping to be useful in defense, Major del Valle joined the enemy camp. Tyrant shouted, "I have nursed vipers!"

And he gave orders for his troops to withdraw to the monastery and left the tower. He asked his barber for a list of suspects and ordered that fifteen be hanged, attempting to curb desertions with that exemplary act. "Does God think a few bums are going to make me give up the ghost! He doesn't know me!"

He was planning to resist for the rest of the day and then to escape under cover of darkness.

IV

In the middle of the morning, the rebels opened fire with their cannons. Soon the way was open for them to attack the bastion. Tyrant Banderas tried to fill the breach, but his troops were deserting and he was forced to retreat to the barracks. Then, assuming his time had come, seeing that his only ally left was his barber, he unbuckled his pistol belt, salivating poisonous, green spittle, and handed it to him. "How sweet it would be if the master chorister were to join us on our journey to Hell!"

Prowling as ever like a snoopy rat, he went to the chambers where he'd shut up his daughter. As he opened the door he could hear demented cries. "Dear daughter, you never married and never became the noble lady that this sinner meant you to be—this sinner who now must take away the life he gave you twenty years ago! It's hardly right you should stay in this world and be enjoyed by your father's enemies, and that they should add insult to injury by calling you the daughter of that Banderas bastard!"

When they heard him, the maids looking after the mad girl pleaded with him desperately to spare her. Tyrant Banderas slapped them in the face. "Bitches! If I let you live, it's because it will be your task to shroud her like an angel."

He took a dagger from his chest, gripped his daughter by the hair to hold her still, and shut his eyes. According to a rebel report, he stabbed her fifteen times.

V

Tyrant Banderas leaned out of the window, waved his dagger, and was shot to pieces. Decapitated by decree, his head was placed on a scaffold in the parade ground for three days in yellow sacking. The same decree ordered that his torso be quartered and scattered from frontier to frontier and from seashore to seashore. Zamalpoa and Nueva Cartagena, Puerto Colorado and Santa Rosa del Titipay were the cities thus blessed.

TITLES IN SERIES

For a complete list of titles, visit www.nyrb.com or write to: Catalog Requests, NYRB, 435 Hudson Street, New York, NY 10014

J.R. ACKERLEY Hindoo Holiday*
J.R. ACKERLEY My Dog Tulip*
J.R. ACKERLEY My Father and Myself*
J.R. ACKERLEY We Think the World of You*
HENRY ADAMS The Jeffersonian Transformation
CÉLESTE ALBARET Monsieur Proust
DANTE ALIGHIERI The Inferno
DANTE ALIGHIERI The New Life
WILLIAM ATTAWAY Blood on the Forge
W.H. AUDEN (EDITOR) The Living Thoughts of Kierkegaard
W.H. AUDEN W.H. Auden's Book of Light Verse
ERICH AUERBACH Dante: Poet of the Secular World
DOROTHY BAKER Cassandra at the Wedding
J.A. BAKER The Peregrine
HONORÉ DE BALZAC The Unknown Masterpiece *and* Gambara*
MAX BEERBOHM Seven Men
STEPHEN BENATAR Wish Her Safe at Home*
FRANS G. BENGTSSON The Long Ships*
ALEXANDER BERKMAN Prison Memoirs of an Anarchist
GEORGES BERNANOS Mouchette
ADOLFO BIOY CASARES Asleep in the Sun
ADOLFO BIOY CASARES The Invention of Morel
CAROLINE BLACKWOOD Corrigan*
CAROLINE BLACKWOOD Great Granny Webster*
NICOLAS BOUVIER The Way of the World
MALCOLM BRALY On the Yard*
MILLEN BRAND The Outward Room*
SIR THOMAS BROWNE Religio Medici *and* Urne-Buriall*
JOHN HORNE BURNS The Gallery
ROBERT BURTON The Anatomy of Melancholy
CAMARA LAYE The Radiance of the King
GIROLAMO CARDANO The Book of My Life
DON CARPENTER Hard Rain Falling*
J.L. CARR A Month in the Country
BLAISE CENDRARS Moravagine
EILEEN CHANG Love in a Fallen City
UPAMANYU CHATTERJEE English, August: An Indian Story
NIRAD C. CHAUDHURI The Autobiography of an Unknown Indian
ANTON CHEKHOV Peasants and Other Stories
RICHARD COBB Paris and Elsewhere
COLETTE The Pure and the Impure
JOHN COLLIER Fancies and Goodnights
CARLO COLLODI The Adventures of Pinocchio*
IVY COMPTON-BURNETT A House and Its Head
IVY COMPTON-BURNETT Manservant and Maidservant
BARBARA COMYNS The Vet's Daughter
EVAN S. CONNELL The Diary of a Rapist
ALBERT COSSERY The Jokers*

* *Also available as an electronic book.*

ALBERT COSSERY Proud Beggars*
HAROLD CRUSE The Crisis of the Negro Intellectual
ASTOLPHE DE CUSTINE Letters from Russia
LORENZO DA PONTE Memoirs
ELIZABETH DAVID A Book of Mediterranean Food
ELIZABETH DAVID Summer Cooking
L.J. DAVIS A Meaningful Life*
VIVANT DENON No Tomorrow/Point de lendemain
MARIA DERMOÛT The Ten Thousand Things
DER NISTER The Family Mashber
TIBOR DÉRY Niki: The Story of a Dog
ARTHUR CONAN DOYLE The Exploits and Adventures of Brigadier Gerard
CHARLES DUFF A Handbook on Hanging
BRUCE DUFFY The World As I Found It*
DAPHNE DU MAURIER Don't Look Now: Stories
ELAINE DUNDY The Dud Avocado*
ELAINE DUNDY The Old Man and Me*
G.B. EDWARDS The Book of Ebenezer Le Page
MARCELLUS EMANTS A Posthumous Confession
EURIPIDES Grief Lessons: Four Plays; translated by Anne Carson
J.G. FARRELL Troubles*
J.G. FARRELL The Siege of Krishnapur*
J.G. FARRELL The Singapore Grip*
ELIZA FAY Original Letters from India
KENNETH FEARING The Big Clock
KENNETH FEARING Clark Gifford's Body
FÉLIX FÉNÉON Novels in Three Lines*
M.I. FINLEY The World of Odysseus
THEODOR FONTANE Irretrievable*
EDWIN FRANK (EDITOR) Unknown Masterpieces
MASANOBU FUKUOKA The One-Straw Revolution*
MARC FUMAROLI When the World Spoke French
CARLO EMILIO GADDA That Awful Mess on the Via Merulana
MAVIS GALLANT The Cost of Living: Early and Uncollected Stories*
MAVIS GALLANT Paris Stories*
MAVIS GALLANT Varieties of Exile*
GABRIEL GARCÍA MÁRQUEZ Clandestine in Chile: The Adventures of Miguel Littín
ALAN GARNER Red Shift*
THÉOPHILE GAUTIER My Fantoms
JEAN GENET Prisoner of Love
ÉLISABETH GILLE The Mirador: Dreamed Memories of Irène Némirovsky by Her Daughter*
JOHN GLASSCO Memoirs of Montparnasse*
P.V. GLOB The Bog People: Iron-Age Man Preserved
NIKOLAI GOGOL Dead Souls*
EDMOND AND JULES DE GONCOURT Pages from the Goncourt Journals
EDWARD GOREY (EDITOR) The Haunted Looking Glass
A.C. GRAHAM Poems of the Late T'ang
WILLIAM LINDSAY GRESHAM Nightmare Alley*
EMMETT GROGAN Ringolevio: A Life Played for Keeps
VASILY GROSSMAN Everything Flows*
VASILY GROSSMAN Life and Fate*
VASILY GROSSMAN The Road*
OAKLEY HALL Warlock

PATRICK HAMILTON The Slaves of Solitude
PATRICK HAMILTON Twenty Thousand Streets Under the Sky
PETER HANDKE Short Letter, Long Farewell
PETER HANDKE Slow Homecoming
ELIZABETH HARDWICK The New York Stories of Elizabeth Hardwick*
ELIZABETH HARDWICK Seduction and Betrayal*
ELIZABETH HARDWICK Sleepless Nights*
L.P. HARTLEY Eustace and Hilda: A Trilogy*
L.P. HARTLEY The Go-Between*
NATHANIEL HAWTHORNE Twenty Days with Julian & Little Bunny by Papa
GILBERT HIGHET Poets in a Landscape
JANET HOBHOUSE The Furies
HUGO VON HOFMANNSTHAL The Lord Chandos Letter
JAMES HOGG The Private Memoirs and Confessions of a Justified Sinner
RICHARD HOLMES Shelley: The Pursuit
ALISTAIR HORNE A Savage War of Peace: Algeria 1954–1962*
GEOFFREY HOUSEHOLD Rogue Male*
WILLIAM DEAN HOWELLS Indian Summer
BOHUMIL HRABAL Dancing Lessons for the Advanced in Age*
DOROTHY B. HUGHES The Expendable Man*
RICHARD HUGHES A High Wind in Jamaica*
RICHARD HUGHES In Hazard
RICHARD HUGHES The Fox in the Attic (The Human Predicament, Vol. 1)
RICHARD HUGHES The Wooden Shepherdess (The Human Predicament, Vol. 2)
MAUDE HUTCHINS Victorine
YASUSHI INOUE Tun-huang*
HENRY JAMES The Ivory Tower
HENRY JAMES The New York Stories of Henry James*
HENRY JAMES The Other House
HENRY JAMES The Outcry
TOVE JANSSON Fair Play
TOVE JANSSON The Summer Book
TOVE JANSSON The True Deceiver
RANDALL JARRELL (EDITOR) Randall Jarrell's Book of Stories
DAVID JONES In Parenthesis
KABIR Songs of Kabir; translated by Arvind Krishna Mehrotra*
FRIGYES KARINTHY A Journey Round My Skull
HELEN KELLER The World I Live In
YASHAR KEMAL Memed, My Hawk
YASHAR KEMAL They Burn the Thistles
MURRAY KEMPTON Part of Our Time: Some Ruins and Monuments of the Thirties
RAYMOND KENNEDY Ride a Cockhorse*
DAVID KIDD Peking Story*
ROBERT KIRK The Secret Commonwealth of Elves, Fauns, and Fairies
ARUN KOLATKAR Jejuri
DEZSŐ KOSZTOLÁNYI Skylark*
TÉTÉ-MICHEL KPOMASSIE An African in Greenland
GYULA KRÚDY The Adventures of Sindbad*
GYULA KRÚDY Sunflower*
SIGIZMUND KRZHIZHANOVSKY The Letter Killers Club*
SIGIZMUND KRZHIZHANOVSKY Memories of the Future
MARGARET LEECH Reveille in Washington: 1860–1865*
PATRICK LEIGH FERMOR Between the Woods and the Water*

PATRICK LEIGH FERMOR Mani: Travels in the Southern Peloponnese*
PATRICK LEIGH FERMOR Roumeli: Travels in Northern Greece*
PATRICK LEIGH FERMOR A Time of Gifts*
PATRICK LEIGH FERMOR A Time to Keep Silence*
PATRICK LEIGH FERMOR The Traveller's Tree*
D.B. WYNDHAM LEWIS AND CHARLES LEE (EDITORS) The Stuffed Owl
GEORG CHRISTOPH LICHTENBERG The Waste Books
JAKOV LIND Soul of Wood and Other Stories
H.P. LOVECRAFT AND OTHERS The Colour Out of Space
DWIGHT MACDONALD Masscult and Midcult: Essays Against the American Grain*
NORMAN MAILER Miami and the Siege of Chicago*
JANET MALCOLM In the Freud Archives
JEAN-PATRICK MANCHETTE Fatale*
OSIP MANDELSTAM The Selected Poems of Osip Mandelstam
OLIVIA MANNING Fortunes of War: The Balkan Trilogy
OLIVIA MANNING School for Love*
JAMES VANCE MARSHALL Walkabout*
GUY DE MAUPASSANT Afloat
GUY DE MAUPASSANT Alien Hearts*
JAMES MCCOURT Mawrdew Czgowchwz*
HENRI MICHAUX Miserable Miracle
JESSICA MITFORD Hons and Rebels
JESSICA MITFORD Poison Penmanship*
NANCY MITFORD Madame de Pompadour*
NANCY MITFORD The Sun King*
HENRY DE MONTHERLANT Chaos and Night
BRIAN MOORE The Lonely Passion of Judith Hearne*
BRIAN MOORE The Mangan Inheritance*
ALBERTO MORAVIA Boredom*
ALBERTO MORAVIA Contempt*
JAN MORRIS Conundrum
JAN MORRIS Hav*
PENELOPE MORTIMER The Pumpkin Eater*
ÁLVARO MUTIS The Adventures and Misadventures of Maqroll
L.H. MYERS The Root and the Flower*
NESCIO Amsterdam Stories*
DARCY O'BRIEN A Way of Life, Like Any Other
YURI OLESHA Envy*
IONA AND PETER OPIE The Lore and Language of Schoolchildren
IRIS OWENS After Claude*
RUSSELL PAGE The Education of a Gardener
ALEXANDROS PAPADIAMANTIS The Murderess
BORIS PASTERNAK, MARINA TSVETAYEVA, AND RAINER MARIA RILKE Letters, Summer 1926
CESARE PAVESE The Moon and the Bonfires
CESARE PAVESE The Selected Works of Cesare Pavese
LUIGI PIRANDELLO The Late Mattia Pascal
ANDREY PLATONOV The Foundation Pit
ANDREY PLATONOV Soul and Other Stories
J.F. POWERS Morte d'Urban
J.F. POWERS The Stories of J.F. Powers
J.F. POWERS Wheat That Springeth Green
CHRISTOPHER PRIEST Inverted World
BOLESŁAW PRUS The Doll*

RAYMOND QUENEAU We Always Treat Women Too Well
RAYMOND QUENEAU Witch Grass
RAYMOND RADIGUET Count d'Orgel's Ball
JULES RENARD Nature Stories*
JEAN RENOIR Renoir, My Father
GREGOR VON REZZORI An Ermine in Czernopol*
GREGOR VON REZZORI Memoirs of an Anti-Semite*
GREGOR VON REZZORI The Snows of Yesteryear: Portraits for an Autobiography*
TIM ROBINSON Stones of Aran: Labyrinth
TIM ROBINSON Stones of Aran: Pilgrimage
MILTON ROKEACH The Three Christs of Ypsilanti*
FR. ROLFE Hadrian the Seventh
GILLIAN ROSE Love's Work
WILLIAM ROUGHEAD Classic Crimes
CONSTANCE ROURKE American Humor: A Study of the National Character
TAYEB SALIH Season of Migration to the North
TAYEB SALIH The Wedding of Zein*
GERSHOM SCHOLEM Walter Benjamin: The Story of a Friendship
DANIEL PAUL SCHREBER Memoirs of My Nervous Illness
JAMES SCHUYLER Alfred and Guinevere
JAMES SCHUYLER What's for Dinner?*
LEONARDO SCIASCIA The Day of the Owl
LEONARDO SCIASCIA Equal Danger
LEONARDO SCIASCIA The Moro Affair
LEONARDO SCIASCIA To Each His Own
LEONARDO SCIASCIA The Wine-Dark Sea
VICTOR SEGALEN René Leys
PHILIPE-PAUL DE SÉGUR Defeat: Napoleon's Russian Campaign
VICTOR SERGE The Case of Comrade Tulayev*
VICTOR SERGE Conquered City*
VICTOR SERGE Memoirs of a Revolutionary
VICTOR SERGE Unforgiving Years
SHCHEDRIN The Golovlyov Family
ROBERT SHECKLEY The Store of the Worlds: The Stories of Robert Sheckley*
GEORGES SIMENON Act of Passion*
GEORGES SIMENON Dirty Snow*
GEORGES SIMENON The Engagement
GEORGES SIMENON The Man Who Watched Trains Go By
GEORGES SIMENON Monsieur Monde Vanishes*
GEORGES SIMENON Pedigree*
GEORGES SIMENON Red Lights
GEORGES SIMENON The Strangers in the House
GEORGES SIMENON Three Bedrooms in Manhattan*
GEORGES SIMENON Tropic Moon*
GEORGES SIMENON The Widow*
CHARLES SIMIC Dime-Store Alchemy: The Art of Joseph Cornell
MAY SINCLAIR Mary Olivier: A Life*
TESS SLESINGER The Unpossessed: A Novel of the Thirties
VLADIMIR SOROKIN Ice Trilogy*
VLADIMIR SOROKIN The Queue
DAVID STACTON The Judges of the Secret Court*
JEAN STAFFORD The Mountain Lion
CHRISTINA STEAD Letty Fox: Her Luck

GEORGE R. STEWART Names on the Land
STENDHAL The Life of Henry Brulard
ADALBERT STIFTER Rock Crystal
THEODOR STORM The Rider on the White Horse
JEAN STROUSE Alice James: A Biography*
HOWARD STURGIS Belchamber
ITALO SVEVO As a Man Grows Older
HARVEY SWADOS Nights in the Gardens of Brooklyn
A.J.A. SYMONS The Quest for Corvo
ELIZABETH TAYLOR Angel*
ELIZABETH TAYLOR A Game of Hide and Seek*
HENRY DAVID THOREAU The Journal: 1837–1861*
TATYANA TOLSTAYA The Slynx
TATYANA TOLSTAYA White Walls: Collected Stories
EDWARD JOHN TRELAWNY Records of Shelley, Byron, and the Author
LIONEL TRILLING The Liberal Imagination
LIONEL TRILLING The Middle of the Journey
IVAN TURGENEV Virgin Soil
JULES VALLÈS The Child
RAMÓN DEL VALLE-INCLÁN Tyrant Banderas*
MARK VAN DOREN Shakespeare
CARL VAN VECHTEN The Tiger in the House
ELIZABETH VON ARNIM The Enchanted April*
EDWARD LEWIS WALLANT The Tenants of Moonbloom
ROBERT WALSER Berlin Stories*
ROBERT WALSER Jakob von Gunten
REX WARNER Men and Gods
SYLVIA TOWNSEND WARNER Lolly Willowes*
SYLVIA TOWNSEND WARNER Mr. Fortune*
SYLVIA TOWNSEND WARNER Summer Will Show*
ALEKSANDER WAT My Century
C.V. WEDGWOOD The Thirty Years War
SIMONE WEIL AND RACHEL BESPALOFF War and the Iliad
GLENWAY WESCOTT Apartment in Athens*
GLENWAY WESCOTT The Pilgrim Hawk*
REBECCA WEST The Fountain Overflows
EDITH WHARTON The New York Stories of Edith Wharton*
PATRICK WHITE Riders in the Chariot
T.H. WHITE The Goshawk
JOHN WILLIAMS Butcher's Crossing*
JOHN WILLIAMS Stoner*
ANGUS WILSON Anglo-Saxon Attitudes
EDMUND WILSON Memoirs of Hecate County
RUDOLF AND MARGARET WITTKOWER Born Under Saturn
GEOFFREY WOLFF Black Sun*
FRANCIS WYNDHAM The Complete Fiction
JOHN WYNDHAM The Chrysalids
STEFAN ZWEIG Beware of Pity*
STEFAN ZWEIG Chess Story*
STEFAN ZWEIG Confusion
STEFAN ZWEIG Journey Into the Past
STEFAN ZWEIG The Post-Office Girl